The Principal's Trial

CHARLES FRANCIS

Contents

Awake

Prologue

⸻ ❧ ⸻

Nestled along the Hudson River, Charles "Chuck" McNab is an Assistant Principal at Todd Jr/Sr High School. With 1,300 students the district has been thinking about building a new building just for the middle school, but they have been saying that for the last 2 years. With it only being a pipe dream, Chuck was ready to move on to Cornel High School. They were impressed with everything he instituted in his building since Sandy Hook. This included safety plans that had a double door system in the front with swap cards, Id badges for all staff, and emergency plans that would effectively go in motion when needed.

His two daughters picked out his outfit for the big interview with the superintendent and board of education. Nicole, the oldest picked a green and yellow tie for the new school colors while the Madison picked out a grey suit to go with a white shirt.

Once everyone was dressed, they drove to the high school so Charles could go into executive council with the his future colleagues. The superintendent had invited the family to witness the formal motion to approval him as the new principal replacing the last one that retired after 22 years at the helm. The district ws proud to have a consistent captain of the ship and Charles had that same type of long vision.

As they were talking he was checking off all the boxes. This included his vision for the building, how he wanted to promote more scaffolding in the classes to meet the needs of all learners, and how he would have COVID. Once the Board starting to discuss the NY Knicks, the superintendent gave Charles a wink. Next, the superintendent offered a salary and Chuck asked for his sick days to carry over from his old district. It was agreed!

The meeting concluded and a board member stated, all we ask is that you keep ELA classes reading only classic novels. Charles smiled and replied that prevents students from seeing other perspectives. We need to build our kids for the global world. They need to have a bicultural component to thrive with others.

The board member was not amused. He called everyone back to discuss the new development. Questions were asked, answers were given, and an informal vote was done in front of the superintendent and Charles. As the first three of the seven votes occurred it was very promising. The forth and fifth board members said "nah". The last two voted "yea". If they voted this way when it was official he would get his first principalship. It just was not sitting right. The superintendent then asked to talk privately. He said he did not like recommending a principal who could not get all "yea" .

He recommended that Charles talk with the two board members which he did. In plain terms he was told that the community was mostly white so stick with Anglo writers. He went back to the superintendent after answering the board members to discuss the next steps. Thinking about it, is it worth being in a place that has this undercurrent? His goal was to be principal.

Alright, it was time to make a decision.

He walked out of the private room, hugged his family, and told Lisa they should enjoy the night. It was a day that would change their life.

Life As Me

Rejection

In our life, we have to make decisions that change the direction of our life. I had the job, but I would rather find this out about their core values now, then as an untenured principal with no control. Well, everything happens for a reason. I guess there is a reason why I am staying here. I better delete the email in my outbox that was going to send to the staff.

Greetings Ladies and gentlemen,

Throughout the last decade, I have been able to work with you to create memories and life-altering experiences for our students. We need to be proud of the accomplishments that have transpired and realize that we can do anything when we are a team. However, we are more than a team. We are a family. I have always believed in treating people with respect. I always believed you do your job to the fullest, without looking for glory. You act as a teammate and people will help you when you need it. I can look at my monitors, TAs, clerical, custodians, support staff, and teachers and say, "You have proven me right on that theory." Todd Jr./Sr. High School has the best academic departments I have ever known and I would be proud to send my children there. When I talk to parents, I frequently used words like "inspiring, outside the box, and will prepare you for life" to illustrate the quality of education that goes on in and out of our classrooms.

Another thing I have appreciated is the fact that Dino allowed me the latitude to do what I knew was in the best interest of our kids and community. He is a great person, friend, and principal.

With that being said,

I will truly miss all the genuine people I have met here.

Always,
Chuck McNab
Assistant Principal

Lately, things have been tough and it has really been a year of unraveling. The pandemic has caused a huge amount of our communities to suffer. Teachers and staff are unhappy. Job cuts looming. I lost my favorite secretary with a 5 minutes notice. Dino might be the type to give me the latitude to do things, but when he gets pissed, he goes for the jugular. Samantha and I don't talk since her promotion. It's as though we don't even know each other. I need to talk to someone to get this off my mind. At least I have my family I can always reach out to. Preferably, I will set up a time to meet with a therapist that Lisa has heard good things about. Maybe there will be some true soul searching and tips on how to improve, but let's hope she does not waste my time discussing my childhood. If it appears to be so, I can easily just walk alone and try to solve my problems one step at a time. Well, let's see how that goes.

"Chuck, you got a phone call. It's Dino," Lisa yelled.

"Hey Dino, what's up?"

"Chuck, I am being told that I am going Christmas shopping tomorrow. If you know what I am saying."

"I hear you."

"So it will be just you and Lauren."

"Why not Sally?"

"Look, people don't know, but she went down to Texas."

"Wait! She went to Texas during this pandemic?"

"Yeah, don't expect to see her for a month. She is taking two weeks off for a Yoga retreat, then she must be quarantined. You both will be fine. There will be no kids tomorrow in the building except special education students. I really need to get this done, Bev will kill me if I think about work. Call me if you need me and maybe I will answer my phone."

"No worries, have a good night, Dino."

"Night brother."

As I hang up, Lisa immediately wanted to know what that was about.

"Chuck, what does Dino want?" Lisa asked

"He is going to be out. That's great, he hasn't taken a vacation for over a year. Everything that is going on has taken a toll on him."

"Yeah, good for Bev to put her foot down as I think that is the only way tomorrow was ever going to happen".

"I am sure it was all Bev."

"I'll touch base with Kathy for tomorrow. It will actually be good having a secretary since I lost mine."

"Chuck, you have to stop harping about that."

"What? I said it is a good thing."

"Chuck, you know what you said. Knock it off. Why don't you ride the Echelon bike to de-stress?"

"By the way, Dino said Sally is in Texas." sighed Charles

"What? No way!" exclaimed Lisa

"Yeah, you know, even as administrators, we can take vacation whenever we want. It is really messed up to take it when school is in session. Taking a vacation for just a day is alright but planning a 2-week vacation in a state that is a hotbed for COVID, you can be sure that she will be out for at least a month."

"Well, you and the crew will have to suck it up and do your best for the kids."

"Yeah, that is it. As for our kids, I'm going to check on Nicole. She has been really quiet. I wonder what she is up to. Then I will go use the bike."

"Alright, I will join Madison for some Just Dance, I'm totally in the mood for Flashdance."

Dr. Dawn

⸎

"Nice to meet you, Charles."

"Same here. Even if it is over zoom."

"Well, we have to take precautions. Those vaccines are just coming out and I am not taking any risk."

"I suppose. I just know this actually cost me more with my insurance than coming in to see you."

"Alright, Charles. Should we get started? What describes you as a person?"

"Hmm...Great family, assistant principal at a junior/senior school, and enjoying baseball and Reese's."

"That sounds good. Usually, people go into detail, but you are short and concise. I am here to help you. Nothing leaves these four walls unless there is someone around or you let it out yourself."

"I know that. My daughters are 5 and 9. My wife is God-sent and amazing. Lisa is a teacher and to hear her in action, I would hope our kids had a teacher like her when they get into high school. She connects Math, which can be a difficult subject for them to cope with. We are living in times that make you realize how valuable family is and I can't see my parents right now except through FaceTime. Recently, my mom had quadruple heart surgery. Although being a trooper, my dad has been supporting her all by himself. School is different....."

"How is school different?

"Really? In a normal year, I would have 1300 students in the hallway. I would tell kids to take off their hoods. I would wish kids a morning hello as I entered their rooms. You would hear the chatter in the cafeteria while kids squeezed to sit at tables, compared to now that they have to sit at desks and you could hear a pin drop. Kids deserve to be kids, not be in a Matilda-like environment."

"That must be very hard to see, especially a principal."

"You have the vision to make the students' lives more successful and it seems academics has gone to the wayside this year with advancements, as we claw our way back to the starting line. I think our kids need mindfulness in their lives. Hell, maybe I need to bring it back into my life as well. We also need to find a way to transpire a single topic that all our kids, staff, and parents can relate to. Last year, the whole school read the book "Restart" by Gordon Korman. We as a community felt compassion, as we were at the edge of our seat page by page. We are a family." Dr. Dawn, do you want it all?"

"Yes, for a first visit, I block in more time to let the flood gates open. For us to have success, for you to experience joy, be connected with your families and friends, and live a meaningful life, we need to discuss the items that are getting in your pathway. There are no straightforward measures to make you happy. We can't skip the hard load. If we do, you will not flourish."

"Over the summer, our superintendent quit. We found out that he never had the certification to be a superintendent. Then, our amazing assistant superintendent was promoted to another district. So, we are left with relatively new people who mean well, but in a normal year would have hard adjustments to our district. It is not fair to them. As a building level administrator, we are getting an endless stream of ever-changing information, or that the teachers' union gets the information before us. This is coupled with the fear and uncertainty of so many unknowns. Will we be open today for students? Will I have to do a contract trace? Which teachers and staff do I need to send home? Which angry parent will I have to deal with because the Department of Health wants them quarantined? Which quarantined child was sent to school anyway? Which of my staff or kids will be the next to get sick? How can I get John Doe to turn on his camera for virtual learning? All of these questions have replaced how will I get the struggling C student to a B? How can I work with this family on attendance? Can I offer more enrichment opportunities for my kids? Dr. Dawn, we are trying to make this abnormal year have some reflection of a normal year. We even had a snow day the other day when our teachers could have worked from home. To get messages of gratitude from parents over having something normal in their children's lives was incredible."

"Charles, what else troubles you? That was a nice sermon, but what affects Charles?"

"Lack of sleep because I am replaying mistakes, missteps, and 'what-ifs' in my head. I mean, the doubts in my head. I have always been insecure about friendships but this year especially, I doubt everyone as a friend. I look at them not just with suspicious eyes, but with inquisitive eyes, wondering if we are really friends. Wondering how they perceived my hello. How awful is that? Doubts if the stairs should be one way or if we should have a lockdown drill because of fear that the kids may be too close. We have only done one this year and instead of going through the whole process, teachers explained what to do instead. How does that help them in a true crisis when we want them to react quickly? How about building up morale while fighting the negative public perception that we are lazy and the only thing we want to do is stay at home. Truth is, we all want to be at work in our school buildings. We want our kids to experience full education. By the way, it is a lot easier teaching the kids in front of you than through a computer, where you have hovering parents watching every moment of each child and hanging on every word a teacher says. Dr. Dawn is that enough to start with?"

"Charles, if you have more, I want to hear it. I want you to unload your stresses. That is the only way to grow and move on."

"I have to be the brave one, pep people up, and assure them everything will work while hiding my own fears and uncertainties. The public puts so much emphasis on an administrator to be perfect, strong, and well adjusted while having no dents in the armor. I have the notion that I am ineffective and cannot promote a positive experience for my kids. I feel lonely and isolated, especially when my secretary took on a new job. I am happy for her, but it went down so very reckless."

"Charles, is there anything positive because of the crisis?"

"Even though people are more negative than ever before, people have been bonding together to support people in crisis. Teachers are learning new methods of promoting education than ever before. There has been a lot of compassion for community members. With all that, it gets easier and easier to stay in one's office."

"Charles, schools are so much more than academics. A school is a place where people come to be loved, feel safe, and be nurtured. That goes for the adults as well. Part of that is you loving and taking it easy on yourself. You are probably your hardest critic. Like it or not, you are the source of stability and calm during the hurricane of life. We need to try and get you a support system though. Just know that a support system is not alcohol, drugs, or you fill in the blank."

"Mine is Peanut butter cups...."

"That sounds great in moderation. Remember, even when you feel like you're failing, you are not. We will continue this next week. While the days move on, if you are feeling stressed, take deep breaths to lower your stress level."

"Thank you, Doc"

"One more thing Charles, our goal is for you to worry more about how you feel about yourself than what your teachers, parents, students, and staff think about you. Once we accomplish that, you will have seen what the majority sees about you."

The Girls

"It's 6:30 and time for a bath."

"Daddy, can I finish this episode of Fuller House?" yelled Nicole.

"How much time is left?"

"7 minutes"

"OK, but straight up afterwards."

"Alright…"

"Daddy, if Nicole is watching Netflix, I can win. I can get done with my bath and dressed before her. Yeah!" exclaimed Madison.

"OK, Madison, it really is not a competition. Any song you want to listen to?"

"Anything by BeBe…you know I love her."

Nicole ran up the stairs and heard I was going to play music for Madison and wanted the same treatment. Just as she would usually say "What you do for one, you do for all."

"Daddy, when I come up, can I listen to Luke Bryan?"

"Sure, you have Google…it can play his songs for you."

For the next 30 minutes, I sang with them and they were funny. I had to do one song with Madison, then raced over to Nicole afterwards. I would have loved to do it together, but they were all in their own bath. The songs have this ability to move us emotionally. Fortunately, the girls do not mind me dancing and demonstrating my vulnerability with my whole body. I could only imagine if my teachers saw me grooving with my arms flailing. I would make Elaine on Steinfeld look good. The music absorbs our attention, acts as a total distraction, and I am suspecting Lisa will start yelling that the girls need to start reading. For me, music is a great aid to meditation and relaxation. It allows my body to unwind from all the stresses of the day. Also, it allows me to bond with my girls. When we are all in the car, for the most part, music prevents the family from fighting. We get that one or two great songs on and the whole fam is singing our hearts out.

"Chuck, are they done with their baths? They need to be reading and settling down," bellowed Lisa from downstairs

"Alright, Nicole. After bath time, get dressed and start reading. Remember we try for 30 minutes each night."

"You know I read more than that. I just finished "Just Jamie" last night after I was tucked in by mommy. By the way, I will need a new flashlight or batteries."

"Why?"

"Well, I was up a lot last night. I went through one and a half books. The Babysitters Club books are just awesome!"

"Hmmm…..let me check on Madison…..your mother will be up soon."

"Madison, let's sing our songs…"

I started to sing itchy, bitsy spider when she said "Daddy, can you put snoopy in front of your face and make him do the dance moves of the song?"

"I would love to."

"Alright baby girl, let's do our famous Eskimo kiss."

"You mean our samosa kiss."

"Ha ha ha….good night princess."

"And don't wake us up."

Still trying to figure out how that tradition started and about her saying it when we used to say it to her. Now, she says it every night.

"Darling, I will see you tomorrow."

"Nicole, are you ready for bed?"

"Daddy, I'm reading the Week Jr….do you think we should have daylight savings time?"

"Good question, what are the pros and cons? What does the magazine say?"

"Daddy, looking at everything they say, I think we should keep it."

"Well, I like it because it provides enough extra light when I am driving and I want to be able to come home to you guys every night."

"Me too daddy, I love you."

3 A.M.

⚜

What is going on? The wind is howling. The patio furniture is blowing everywhere. Time to turn on the iPad and check out what the weather would say. 30mph winds and heavy rain. I guess I would rather have a heavy rain than snow at this point of the year. I ran out of driveway salt with the last winter blast. My spotlights outside keep going off and it must be because of the rain. I hope the neighbors don't get too upset. Shit, what is the beeping? Will the fire alarm go off? No, it's the security system that is supposed to be disabled. Why is it going off? Back to the iPad to figure this out. Alright, press the * button and it will turn off. OK, since I am up, it would be easy to knock out some emails. The first email is that of a parent demanding to go remote from hybrid so it won't ruin the holiday break. Easy fix. The second email is that of a special education coordinator who wants to move a 8th grader from Inclusion to a social-emotional special class that only houses 9th and 10th graders. Dwight, what are you thinking? The teacher isn't certified to teach 8th grade and that would mean the teacher would have to teach 3 grades level time 4 curriculums. I wouldn't wish that on my worst enemy, let alone an untenured teacher. Alright, write back to me and shed light on the situation. I totally get that the parent is abrasive, but the current special education teacher needs to talk and work things out with her. Don't dump a bad situation on a newbie. The third email stems from a teacher who is losing all of her virtual teams and refusing to teach unless it comes back on. I will let her know that the technology department will be involved. The fourth email is a parent's complaint about a teacher who ignores students' questions and is teaching fre-

shaman like a college lecture course in the classroom. This is the first year this teacher has been like this. I think she is burnt out in the classroom, especially as she does everything virtually. However, the parents are watching from home and are critical about every step we take with our kids. She has always been a fantastic teacher. In regard to that, I need to kindly address the issue with the teacher and have her call the parent. The problem is that a lot of our teachers believe that if they email their concerns it is considered as contacting a guardian. How do we know if the email address is still valid? Calling not only gets immediate feedback, but people can sense the correct tone over the phone instead of interpreting why something is capitalized or not. The next email is from a parent stating that our system shows the child has been absent for 20 days and she is claiming that her child has only been out four times. The dad requests an immediate meeting to rectify the situation. It's 3:15 and I am finally getting to the last email before I try to fall back asleep. Advice on social-emotional strategies can be done in the classroom because I hear the pillow calling my name.

Driving to Work

C an't believe that just happened. Really? The babysitter cancels again? L wants me to stay home, but Dino has already called out. I have sucked it up quite a bit. I am so hoping my parents were able to help, or I will be turning the car around. I just wished my daughters were lucky enough to get more than a day in school. I know the district is trying, but when parents are paying $150 a day for a babysitter while already paying taxes, something has to be given. Plus I don't get a stimulus check because we have decent jobs. The government should factor in all the extra payments we need to make so that we can keep our decent jobs. Add, angering my wife because she is probably going to kill me when I get home tonight. You know what? When I get to work, if my calendar isn't too full, maybe I will try to only do a half-day. I will call Dino after the morning announcements. I think I will text Lisa to let her know about it instead of getting into another fight. "A Long December" is playing on the radio. I love this song and it is so fitting for the year that we are having. I want to call Ken before I get into the office, let's hope it doesn't go to his voicemail.

"Morning Ken".

"How are you bud?"

"Doing well. Driving to work. No kids today except special education students as we are semi-remote. A kid tested positive yesterday and with all the tracing, we had to send home 10 staff members."

"It is getting unreal. I had to send 5 home yesterday as well."

"The parties that the students are having have caused a major spread."

"Did you guys find out if the parents knew about the last party?"

"Parents claim they did not know, as they were out of town enjoying the good life in Cape Cod. They said their son promised just to focus on his schoolwork and was to change the oil of the car."

"Do you believe them?"

"Not for me to say."

"So what's up for the day?"

"Well, making sure our staff took the COVID screener and looking at next year's budget. There are going to be a lot of cuts. The state hasn't given us our aid yet. We are in the hole by millions, and if this type of learning continues, parents are going to start protesting since they all want their children in school. Guess what, I get it. I want my kids in school as well."

"Chuck, at my school, they are in. Yesterday, I had a freshman throw a desk and say to the teacher how they screwed the teacher's mom so hard that she won't be able to walk for a month. They are getting younger and younger with more social-emotional issues. As I was talking with the kid, he lifted his shirt so that he could play with his fat stomach like a drum."

"Ummm….Ken..glad you dealt with that instead of me. Look, it isn't just the kids, it's the employees as well. We have a lot of fun at our school. However, one person took it too far. He put a giant unicorn bumper sticker on the patrol car that is parked in front of our school. The shit rolled down from there.

"It's 2020, everything is turned upside down."

"Look, Ken, I am pulling up at the school. I have to cancel my meetings in the morning since Dino and Sally are out and our SRO is going to one of the elementary schools to visit the staff. I want to be visible to our staff and let them know someone is here."

"Wait…Why is the SRO doing that? I thought all your schools had police officers."

"Well, the younger schools have safety officers, but they were furloughed to help with the budget. I will talk to you later."

"Oh OK, my brother. You have fun."

As I pull into my administrator parking spot, there are only a few cars here. It is still dark, about 19 degrees and I need to find my mask. Do I go with Reese's peanut butter one or Goofy? Instead, I decided to put on the Hard Rock Christmas lights as a reminder that this is the week before the holiday recess. As I open my Baby Blue Subaru Outback's door I am reminded of how this car saved my life on this very day last year. It is not the first time getting at the reared end in Poughkeepsie or getting hit by an 18-wheeler on 84, but my Suub has always kept me safe.

I see a teacher in the parking lot singing the Bonanza show tune.

"Hi Liz, hope you are having a great day so far."

"Chuck, I am. Today we are using math to have an ugly sweater drawing contest. If you get a chance, would you stop by one of my classes to see their progress? The kids love having you in the room, even if it is virtual."

"I will definitely try. I have some observations on the calendar but let me see what I can do. Remember to do your COVID screener."

As I walk into the main office, Jan is taking the attendance. She explains how we have six teachers out for quarantine, apart from the three that reported sick, and one out for personal reasons. The one who was out for personal reasons seems to love her Fridays off.

"Jan, are you doing anything fun this weekend?"

"Well, besides trying to sell this one home and showing some clients houses in the area, I will spend some time with my grandkids. I want to see them before the next snowstorm on Monday."

"I forgot about the storm; it can bring 8 inches. Fortunately, I bought a snowblower, so the girls don't have to freeze out there with me as much."

Immediately, I began to think to myself, how did we get to snow already? This year has been one big blur of Zoom meetings, COVID tracing, and giving bad news…March turned into July which then turned into December. Even when I took a vacation day, I was in zooms…need this to go back to old normal. I want to see our kids, see their actual smiles and not mask, and watch them get set in our routines.

Jan looked back up from her computer screen and continued with the conversation. "Chuck, this will be the first time Ted would let me be with the boys since he is afraid of them getting sick. I need to follow all the same protocols as we do here. Ted is my favorite son but get real. I don't think these masks can prevent me from getting or receiving COVID from my grandkids if they had it."

"Jan, I would look at our rates. The kids and staff that tested positive did not get it from our school. Most of them got it from soccer, field hockey, and ice hockey. Others got it from their families or parties. Poor Mr. Wilson got it at church."

"Alright, I am going to look at my calendar. Tell Kathy she can come into the office whenever she wants. Thank you, Jan."

As I was about to open my calendar, I saw a hand and two eyes peeking in. "Hi Chuck, I was wondering if my son can take his picture with me on picture day. I know the students are supposed to do it at night, but honestly, I don't have time for that. If I could pull him out of class while I have lunch to let him take the picture, that would be awesome."

"Melvin, you want to pull your son out of his English class so that he can take his picture with you? Isn't he failing English?"

"Yeah, but Ms. Brown won't mind. If it makes you feel better, I will tell the other teachers that you want me to cut the line to get Ralph back to class."

"Melvin, let me get this straight. You are asking me to let your son, who is failing, out of his worst class to take pictures with the rest of the teachers. We aren't allowing any other parent this choice and you think it is a good idea?"

"I do. My time at home matters and I wish you could see that. Instead of asking all these questions, it would have been easier for you just to say yes so we can move on with our day."

"Sorry, Melvin, I can not do that. If you are too busy tonight to take him, ask your husband to take him. If he isn't able to, I know we will have retake night in a couple of weeks."

He leaves in a huff. I started looking at my calendar and noticed that I have my physical right after school. This 41-year-old body better not fail me today. Doc will say again, Chuck you have to find a way to relieve stress. I will joke about the gray hair in my goatee and raising two girls and a wife who is stressed teaching remotely from home. So with the job I have, how can I find the time? I bet it will be until February before I can even get my blood work done because I need creamer in my coffee to start my day from all the lack of sleep.

Just as I am venting to myself about the physical, Kathy walks in.

"Chuck, morning. Do you want to get straight to business or hear about my day last night?"

"Did you finish your quilt?"

"Yes! It is all set for the fundraiser. I think it can really help the camp."

"Did you also make some mask?"

"I made a St. Bonaventure mask for you if that was what you were hinting at. I think though I am going to stop making them since they are ready in stock anywhere you go. Alright, we can talk more later, but you had several messages last night. Colette is asking if you found a way to get Bluetooth headsets to replace the corded headsets that she feels the district office really screwed up on buying. Next, the new superintendent wants to meet with you on zoom today to ask you about the budget. Third, Jim called to question why you need a bi-lingual clerical instead of a regular clinical. It will cost an extra $1.75 an hour to make the change. The last message was from Mr. Holbrook, questioning why we are using a 60-passenger bus if only 4 kids get on it."

"Alright, work with the calendar to find times for me to call Jim at the district office and have the zoom meeting. I want to call the PTA about the headsets. I will call Mr. Holbrook after the morning announcements. Also, please find time for Liz Peck's class today. I still have to hand out gifts to the staff. I am going to try and sit in the hallway to be visible as well."

"Will do and don't forget that when Deputy Hunter is back, he wants to talk about Table Top drills…he was hinting that he would like to play out a bomb threat with the safety team."

"Thank you Kathy and by the way, your tea smells delicious."

8:00 AM

⚮

On the P.A. "Good morning Falcons and thank you for standing during the pledge for home and in-person! Here is your announcements today. Next week we are hoping we will all be back in school. We are also doing spirit week. Please look in your emails for each day's theme. Remember, if you have any food to donate to the food bank, please put it outside of the main lobby. We will bring the food to the food bank twice a week. Happy birthday to Juan Peters, he is turning eleven today. After announcements, I will stop by in every class to say hello either virtually or in-person."

"Chuck, there are a lot of people donating food today. It is really awesome. Maybe you should go out there and take a picture and tweet it. The community would love to see the outreach," remarked Kathy.

"You are right, Kathy. That's an excellent idea. Once I finish the hellos, I will go out."

"Chuck, Michele would like you to say hello to her class today. They have something special to show you."

"Alright, I will have her class as the last class today, so I can give her as much time as she wants."

I went from class to class and said hi starting with all the virtual classes. The faces were ones of bittersweet. They were happy to be in a class, but not happy to be out of the building. What are we supposed to do? The infection rate in the county is over 8%. The last thing we want is for someone to get seriously sick. I went to Mrs. Frederick's class where they wanted to challenge me to a game, "bet you are not as smart as a 8th grader". I was doing pretty well until they asked the capital of Idaho. I said Bismarck and a bunch of my kiddos actually got the answer right. As a former social studies teacher, I felt slightly embarrassed but proud of them for getting it right. The capital of Idaho should be called Potato. I'm just saying that it is the only thing I think about when I think of Idaho.

Once I signed off on Zoom, I grabbed some Cinnabon coffee. And since my watch messaged me that it was time to stand up, I thought walking around the school to the in-person classes would be a great thing to do. I started in the 10th grade wing, went past the nurses down through the cafeterias, and then back up the stairs near the front lobby. I got a fifth of the building done.

As I was walking towards the entrance of the school, I was notified that a strange person was coming up to the school. I was told he was wearing a black hoodie and ripped jeans. I went to the main office knowing he could not get into the building since he would either have to scan a card or check-in with the greeter. He did end up buzzing the greeter and she asked him who he was and his reason for being here.

His reasons shifted from being there to pick up his child in 4th grade to picking up work, then to needing a meeting with the nurses. This set off alarms as people know that our kids in our building start from 7th grade. I went to the camera feed and took a snapshot of his face.

From there, I sent the picture to Deputy Hunter. He called me right away saying he was getting another deputy there immediately since there is a restraining order on Mr. West, who is the ex-husband of one of our 8th grade teachers. With that being said, I immediately called for a lockout. A lockout is when no one is permitted to either leave or come into the building.

Mr. West is starting to look angry and pacing really quickly. Then, he turns around and starts to go down the stairs. Just then, a bus driver pulls up and comes up the stairs to probably come in to use the bathroom. I race to the lobby to prevent her from coming in, but it is too late. Mr. West had followed her in, in fact, the bus driver held the door for him. How many times have we told the staff not to allow people to enter the building with you? What a hard lesson we will now encounter. Why did her scan card work if we had a lockout going on?

Now, Mr. West and I are in the lobby. The bus driver went straight for the restroom and the greeter went into the main office to let the district office know what is going on. I also instructed her to call a lockdown if anything should go wrong.

"Hi, Mr. West what are you doing here?"

"How do you know my name? Are you stalking me?"

"It is my job to know who enters the building sir. Again, what are you doing here?"

"I am here to see my wife."

'I am sorry sir, but she is absent today. Maybe you can call her when you get back into your car."

"Her car is in the parking lot. I should know as I bought her the BMW last Christmas. I still make the payments as part of our....he paused. Why did you lie to me? I want to talk with her right now."

"Sir, I might have made a mistake, but if she is here and it is 9:00, then she is teaching."

"Well, I will go up and surprise her."

"Sorry, but you cannot go up. In fact, I need you to leave if you are not here for school-related business."

"I need to speak with her. It is important and I will not leave until I do."

"Just then, the PE department came over to help me out. The wrestling coach looked eager to put him in a headlock."

"Sir, I am asking one more time for you to leave before I get the SRO involved."

"HA! He isn't here. His car is not in his normal parking spot. He leaves at this time. I have noticed this the last few days."

Has this guy been checking out our school? What is going on right now? With that last statement, I dialed the emergency number on my cell phone that was in my back pocket. I tried my best for the dispatcher to hear the name of our school and what was going on. In the background, I could hear the police sirens. He was shocked by the noise and turned around. At that time, one of the coaches tried to tackle him, but he noticed. He pulled out a handgun and hit the coach with the bullet in the shoulder. It sounded like a balloon popping. Such a tiny object will impact our school and community forever. The next time the coach wears his favorite Syracuse University sweatshirt, will it bring him joy or rush sudden flashbacks to today? The next time this happens, God forbid, will the coach rethink his options? Would he hide in a closet, jump out a window for safety, or come help again when he believes the school is in danger?

Sam, one of my other coaches was flexing a baseball bat and shouted "We will go down fighting". Mr. West did not look frightened; he was more agitated and confused. He started shouting that he wanted his wife and that he would leave after that. I told Sam and the others to attend to Duke and get him to the nurse's office. Mr. West was alright with that. Maybe he was remorseful…or at least I hoped.

The coach was shaken up since the power of the bullet knocked him down. The other coaches were just staring at Duke but then walked over to him to lift him up. He got his cell phone out and immediately, Mr. West told him to put it away. As this was happening, I pressed the talk button on my walkie-talkie. I was praying that none of the monitors would talk as I really could not change channels. My goal was to hope that either the main office or Lauren can hear what was going on. Maybe one of them could call for an ambulance just in case my idea of having my phone on in my back pocket doesn't work. I know it is an afterthought, but maybe one of them would call Duke's family to let them know that he is injured. What am I thinking? At this point, random calls like that can not happen. Getting an ambulance was really needed. Maybe 911 heard it on my phone, if it wasn't muffled. In any case, Lauren or the main office would call for an immediate lockdown. Duke did put the phone away and the other coaches picked him up and walked away very fast; imagine walking fast and carrying 250 pounds of muscle to the nurse's office.

Great timing, but as they rounded the corner, Lauren was on the PA to call for a lockdown. You could hear the slight panic in her voice. We weren't trained for this in admin 101. We went into this for the love of the kids. You can hear all the classroom doors getting slammed and then, there was an eerie silence. I was just thinking to myself "This can't be happening in our school." At the same time, I was proud of all our training throughout the years. Our teachers got this. They will protect our kids. I was snapped back into reality when Mr. West said, "You are my ticket out of here." He was pissed and pointed his gun at me.

"Sure, no problem. Just don't hurt anyone else." He asked me to open the door. I did as instructed and he motioned to his white Nissan Pathfinder. It was pretty banged with a front light broken and scratches down the passenger's side. As we got through the first door of the man trap, he mentioned that he had a change of heart. He desperately wanted to go see his ex. I tried to persuade him that we should go before the police arrived. Maybe if he could get over the New York border into Westport, he could get lost in the weeds. From Westport, he could hop on the Metro North to Penn Station and Amtrak could take him wherever he wanted. Yeah, I might have talked a little too much as he was getting enraged now. In fact, I learned the hard way to keep my mouth shut because just then he shot me in the leg to make me keep quiet. Mr. West then cautioned me to quit my moaning or my other leg would be shot as well and he would go to the nurse's office for his next hostage. His next directive was to take him to his wife's classroom. I complied. As I was limping and he was walking, he reminded me who was in charge by holding the gun behind my back.

"Mr. Maxwell get in a room now, this is not a drill." Even when it is the real thing, some teachers will not listen or think they are above the rules. Mr. West made a snickering remark to the effect that the guy and his ex should hook up because they both think they are hot shit. As he was saying that, a boy was running so fast in a distance. He ran so fast that he became blurred. He must have come from the bathroom and was trying to desperately go into his class. He was banging on the door, but they won't let him in. Honestly, good for the teacher. That is what we train to do. I yelled at the boy to go through the exit at the end of the hallway and wait there for help. He seemed reassured, but nervous. I yelled at him again, "Tell your parents I said hello." He knows that is something I would say and run to the exit. Mr. West sarcastically said, "You know I wouldn't have blasted a kid." I didn't reply, because I was afraid to get shot again. I just started to pray that I would see my kids and beautiful wife again.

We are a distance away from the front now and you could hear the glass of the doors being cracked open. We got to the stairs and you can see through the window panes the Sheriffs, Troopers, and the Brewster PD swarming the building. Why couldn't they see us? They could have a clean shot if I just ducked. They were looking straight ahead, but sometimes in life, you need to look up. I tried to convince Mr. West to give up and end it peacefully, but he was determined to see my teacher, his ex. I even started to say she isn't worth it and that he could do better. He reminded me that she was his cash cow. They can easily live on her salary while he was a stay-at-home dad. When they separated, she still had to support him. Their son went to her though, even though Mr. West said she was the unfaithful one. I think I recall that she had an affair with an administrator or a custodian. It was so petty that I really did not give it a second thought. Externally though, I had no words. Whatever I said at the moment probably would not help the situation. I was just moments away from getting to the top of the stairs and his ex had the max allowed of students in her room. I couldn't bear witness to Johnny, Jose, or the rest of the kids seeing someone get injured. The trauma that they would have could shatter them. I wonder what I could do. He was breathing hard just as though climbing the stairs was a struggle. It could be from what I suspected; that he was drunk. Then I had an idea from the drunk thought. I stumbled on the stairs and fell back into him. Maybe not the wisest thing, but I couldn't risk anymore more lives. He was startled and fell back as well while cursing like a sailor. Then a loud bang went off. This was not ideal for me as he fired a shot before the gun slipped out of his hand. I felt the bullet rip my skin open, but I was more concerned about catching the gun. With my left hand, I caught the handgun in mid-flight and discharged a round into his stomach. I plunge to the floor and started to roll down the stairs. Now everything started to become a fog.

The Sheriffs arrived at the stairwell and immediately called for three ambulances. I can't see anything, but I heard other officers scream to check the rooms and get everyone out of the building. I heard someone shouting to get a medic and even the nurses at the stairwell.

"Chuck, it's Carol. You look good Chuck. I have some gauze that I am going to use to stop the bleeding. Chuck, I texted Kathy to call your wife. You will be OK. I will get you patched up before the medic arrives."

"Why are you working on him?" shouted Carol to the medic. "You need to be over here helping the principal. He is losing a lot of blood. Hurry."

"Ma'am, we help all injured, no matter if they are the perp or the victim."

"Well, the principal has been shot twice and I think we are losing him."

What did she mean by we are losing him? I thought she was patching me up.

Another medic rushed over to me. "We need to get him to the hospital right away. Mr. McNab, can you hear me?"

I was trying to shout yes, but for some reason, they didn't hear me.

"Mr. McNab, Mrs. McNab....get the AED."

We need it now. I heard someone yell that we should move out of the way that the stretcher is coming. Then I heard someone asking, "Which hospital?" The medic replied "The local county one." I heard them gasp and I knew I needed Vassar.

Platform

I don't know what is going on. I hear screams, but I see blue. The hallway with all the student work hanging flickers in and out. Then, without notice, all I see is new to me. I check my body and I am completely fine. Maybe, what just happened was a dream, but could I have had a dream within a dream? Then I thought maybe I am in heaven. The Steve Martin movie and the other guy pops into my heaven. Wow, I still remember going to that movie in Peekskill with my parents. The title of the movie was 'My Blue Heaven'. The song is blasting in my head and I'm trying to sing it, but as my wife always said, I could never get the lyrics right.

Now, I need to figure out where I am. I look around and there are only clouds as far as I can see. If this is heaven, they need to put up some signage. Then in the far distance, I could see something sparkling. I walk over and it was a gate with someone checking people in and handing out tickets. I remind myself that it is not time for stupid jokes when I get up there. Sometimes, when I am nervous I can put my foot in my mouth. Finally, it is my time up at the counter. It reminds me of one of the old subway customer service stations. It is a box with a speaker to talk through. Only, in this case, the speaker is not muffled, as there is not any graffiti and it looks as new as can be. I only wonder why the person needs to be in a box. If this is heaven, everyone should be nice, right?

I said hello and found that his nametag says Michael. He was not a person though, but an angel. The wings were so beautiful. So many movies depicted the wings right. They weren't pure white, but almost the color of the wings in "Angel in Centerfield" with a dirty brown color blending in with the white. He asked me for my name to cross-reference with the screen. There was no keyboard, but somehow he was able to get the screen to switch displays. Since I wasn't Tec savvy, I asked him how he was able to get that done and he said it was controlled by his mind. He looked at one list that was labeled the "H" train, but my name was not there. I started to sweat, wondering if I was not going to heaven. What could I have possibly have done? I never cheated on my wife, I treated my kids with love and spent my life devoted to helping children learn and become successful. I thought about it some more and the only thing I could think of was that I did not go to church. Would that make me spend the rest of my time in the fiery pits of hell? I started to sweat, feeling the fake heat toasting my skin. Michael went to the next list for the "P" train. I could not figure out what the "P" stood for, but could only think of "prison". Who knows, maybe God had a special name for hell that no one knew. Saint Michael looked confused and opened a new program. It was a database on every person born. As he was moving from person to person, I saw my brother's name with it labeled as active. Then the screen had my name listed, but it was actually a person with the same name as mine, but a comedian from England. His name said active as well. Finally, my name and picture appeared. Next to my name was listed "error". That just brought up a lot of questions in my head. Was I an error? I have heard of accidents or surprise babies, but an error? Fortunately, I was not the only one confused with this. All of the sudden, Michael touched his ear and asked for St. Augustine to open another booth at the gate. Was I really talking to St. Michael? This was awesome, but why did they have to open another booth? What was going on with my name? Where am I supposed to go? Maybe there was a chance to go to heaven after all. I asked him what this means and he said that it is rare to have this error and joked we are human after all. It was nice to see there was humor up here. Wherever here was.

St. Michael touched his ear again. That was when he asked me to come back in 5 minutes and I replied 'alright.' I soon realized that I did not have a watch on and my cellphone did not seem to have reception. As I had my phone out, it was an impulse to check my text messages, Facebook, and emails. Several text messages must have appeared before my phone was disabled.

From George: Dude are you OK? Call me.

From Steve: Chucky, call me. Heard there was an issue at your school.

From Lisa: Babe, talk to me. What is going on? My AP told me there was an issue.

From Bonnie: Umm, Charlie, why the hell is the superintendent giving robocalls that the school is closed?

From Ken: Why do my special need students need busing so early in the day to leave the school?

I don't remember what had happened. I just remember being in the hallway and then being here. As I looked around, I saw a line of people that I did not notice before approaching the gate. There were people of all types; from all over the world. Some dressed in their religious garbs. At the end of the day, we all get judged by the same values and are all welcomed in heaven or hell.

As I walked back to the booth, St. Michael, as I probably should be referring to him, gave me the signal to hold on as he wrapped up the call. I looked at the pictures on my phone. My little girl made some funny faces on my phone prior to me leaving for work. She was always very silly. How many times did we tell her not to put her fingers in her mouth and yet, she does. I stumbled upon one of my favorite pictures of the family on the beach. That was a glorious summer. We were all smiling, not knowing what the world was going to bring us a few months later. COVID has laid havoc. So many people who should not have died were all dead because people ignored wearing masks or obey the social distance rules. St. Michael asked me to approach. He told me St. Francis would help me the rest of the way. It is amazing that all the saints were now angels. I suppose they were angels on Earth as well, just not physically apparent.

St. Francis asked how I was doing and I explained that I was confused. I had no clue where I was and why I was there. He explained that I was at the gate of the train platform. Michael had two lists prefilled with all reservations. However, my reservation was not available. The research department did a quick scan of my records and determined I should go on the "P" train. I was thinking and must have said it out loud, "Why not the "H" train". He asked why I would want to go to hell. I must have looked dumbfounded as he chuckled and said the "H" stands for hell. I was thinking in my mind, shit, I am glad they did not honor my request. St. Francis, where does the "P" train take you? He answered, "To purgatory." That is great! I am in limbo. Looking around, I noticed there were 4 train platforms. One listed as "H", one listed as "P", one listed as "E", and another listed as "D". Both the "E" and the "D" were a lot smaller platforms. St. Francis must have known what I was thinking and said "E" was express to heaven. Not many people have an express trip there; there are always questions and research needed. Then he said he would not explain nor would anyone explain what the "D" train was. He said, "Only when the time was right would someone of authority explain it."

The platforms were filling fast. There were a lot of people on both the "P" and "H" platforms. Both had people in suits, old grannies, bikers, regular folk in jeans, etc. While we were ready to board, I could hear a man in a suit jacket say to an elderly lady with a purse, "Aren't you on the wrong platform?" She responded that she deserved hell since she robbed a bank and grocery store. St. Francis then whispered in my ear, "You cannot judge a book by its cover."

Soon, two sleek trains arrived; one read with a lightning bolt and another green with flowers. They were hovering at the platforms. Conductors came out from both to check tickets. A certain guy who was looking quite presidential with a lot of makeup on then tried to run over the tracks to get on the green train. He must have stepped on the invisible 3rd rail as he started to get buzzed frequently. He screamed, "I have been framed. This was rigged." He reminded me of someone, but I couldn't put my finger on it. Most people boarded the green train or the "P" train with a smaller percentage on the "H" train.

St. Francis ushered me onto the train and explained that he will escort me the entire way to my next designation. It was a quick ride. It was almost like a blink of the eye, but on the train platform, we were just nowhere to be seen. I have made it to purgatory or limbo.

It was beautiful though, with people smiling, some others nervous. Some people had escorts with blue suits and shoulder bags. I began wondering who they were and what my next step was.

Purgatory

Purgatory Campus

In purgatory, it looked like a lot of buildings nestled onto this property. St. Francis pointed to the building with a beautiful gold fountain of Mary. I figured that had to be a good sign. The building was white with gold trim around the windows. As I walked into the building, I was greeted by the marble floors. People dressed up in the 1920's attire lined up against the wall to help. The red-suited bellhops were so polite. If you passed, they would each say hello. How does a person become a bellhop or an employee in purgatory? Shouldn't they enjoy the same fate as everyone else, whether in heaven or hell? St. Francis wished me farewell as I stepped up to the counter. The hotel must have been expecting me as they already knew my name. I was pretty sure they knew that since St. Francis was escorting me, it was for a reason. They had my reservation listed which was a sense of relief. However, it was listed "to be determined" for the of number of days. That was not a thrilling concept to not have the foggiest idea of how many days I would be spending. They explained that I was booked in a private condo off to the side of the hotel. It was freshly cleaned and had a hot tub. One of the bellhops would walk me to the room. I asked for a key and the manager said my thumb would open the door. Before I left the counter I said "You know, I haven't fully lived". The manager said you should have lived life fully each day. Point taken. Those days on my cellphone or iPad could have been devoted to my family.

As the bellhop walked me around the hotel, he suggested I avoid the west wing. He said those people booked over there are usually not the friendliest and have pretty quick decisions. I was intrigued with what he said and asked him to clarify. He explained that people who are not on the express train to heaven, which is usually most of the people, go before a panel of judges to determine if they will proceed to heaven or not. Wow, I wondered if I would get any help to plan my defense. But what do I have to defend? That I stuck a peanut up my brother's nose? I paid heavily for it with the guilt and shame. Then, I noticed that these hallways are so long. I asked the bellhop how many rooms this hotel has and he explained that the numbers always shift. During a pandemic or horrible storm, thousands of rooms will appear overnight. The office gets a new map layout and shares with the staff. Generally, we know where the extra rooms are going to be located. In a rare case, floors will be added to the hotel. Since most people do not stay more than a week, they will never know that the hotel has changed. "What about the people that come back from being dead?" I wondered. He said that is so rare, but he had it from a good source that they don't remember much of their experience here. However, he compared it to a couple who have vacations at the same hotel for 20 years. They wouldn't know the exact changes, they would just know if the place has been kept to standards.

Finally, we were in the room. It was beautiful. It was spacious and overlooked one of the most beautiful scenes I can remember from my honeymoon. We were at the Hard Rock Hotel in Biloxi, Mississippi. It overlooked the Gulf of Mexico and the sunsets were magnificent. I called the lobby and asked if this was the scene out of every room and they said no, that it rotates between scenes that were most precious on one's mind. That got me thinking about the births of my girls, the hotel room overlooking the renewing of my vows, and the falling stars as I laid on the White Sand Desert in Egypt. At least, that was what I predicted for possible scenes. The room itself did not represent anything from my past. However, it was sleek, almost all white, no pictures even though that would have been a nice touch. But it had sculptures that captivated the mind. There was no kitchen and the bathroom was modest.

There was a television that welcomed me to the hotel. Funny enough, the hotel had no name. It had a check-in date, but not a check-out date listed. The television was unique because one channel was devoted to me. I could watch my life by the year. There was no editing and it allowed me to watch the movie from different perspectives. I really wish I could have had that ability when I was alive. I decided to look at my elementary years and I didn't realize that I had that many friends. The biggest thought that ran through the screen was that of one of my classmates who had tan skin but keeps denying he is Hispanic. I denied I was Hispanic because I wasn't. I was Indian. I also did not realize I was made fun of a lot of times on the soccer field because I always throw up after running a couple of feet. It took till 4th grade to find out the problem, but people always associated me with throwing up. It is almost like Karma because I, with a couple of others, always made fun of a girl who was relieving herself in her pants. If you could only turn back time, you could make things right. Next, I went to my middle school years. I was quite shy and always felt odd that I was not rich since it was a private school. However hearing the other perspectives, no one questioned my wealth. The girl I had a crush on had wanted me to ask her out. My biggest embarrassment was when my parents made me dress in my school uniform for the dance. However, a lot of my peers went through a similar experience in earlier grades. It is funny how you feel like you are the only one who experiences unique issues, but they happen more than we think. My science teacher who had a tough exterior shell actually considered all of us as her kids since she could not have any on her own. She loved all of us.

Judicial Building

⟢

The next morning, I woke up to knocking on the door. I must have fallen asleep on the couch and my 30's were playing on the television. I still had last night's clothes on when I opened the door. There was a note in the bellhop's hand that stated that I should be in the lobby in an hour to meet a particular Ms. Jenkins. Questions came to my mind such as, do I shower, do I have clothes to wear, and where do I get a toothbrush? Do you smell? Can your gums rot? Am I becoming that 7-year-old boy who thinks he can just sprinkle some water on his face and is all set? Or the 7-year-old who forgets to brush his teeth the day the dental hygienist visits and has everyone chew a pill to help them see where they missed brushing in his/her mouth? To play it safe, I will call the lobby. Another question popped into my head. Who is Ms. Jenkins?

The lobby explained that if I pop into the bathroom and push the button in the shower, it will automatically refresh. It was amazing that my goatee automatically was trimmed, I smelled clean, and my teeth were minty. As an added bonus, I was automatically dressed in the outfit I was thinking in my head. This would save a lot of time on Earth. I wonder if people still skip this function here. I left my room to go to the lobby. Every time I thought I would get lost, an arrow would appear. It was just as though God could sense that I needed help. On a white couch between two palm trees sat a lady in a blue suit with a briefcase. She noticed me at once and welcomed me to the area. She asked if I wanted to go to the business room or take a walk outside. I asked how the weather was and she said it is always sunny here. "Let's go for a walk to the judicial building," she said.

I did not really notice the sights because I was glued to every word she stated about the process. She corrected me when I said she will defend me. She said that is not the word they use here, instead they use "advocate" in place of the word I had mentioned earlier. There will be opposing counseling and depending on who you get, it can really impact the outcome. Finally, the major areas they discussed are courage, honesty, compassion, how you treat others, and your sins.

"Do I need to think of events that showed those virtues?"

"You may, but, I have a team that goes over your whole life. This way, we are prepared on both sides of the fence. Just like how you were watching "This is your life" channel last night, they have been watching the same channel since you came up here. They also have a special code to find certain events instantly. Just remember that opposing counsel has the same features."

"Now, we plan on calling witnesses to the stand. So far, we are bringing back your Grandpa, Tonja Bathe, Aunt Kathy, and Willy. As of right now, I do not know who the opposing side will bring. They can bring up five people. Reviewing your case, I do not see any glaring, deal-breaking holes that I am worried about. However, I do not know what angle they are going to attempt. I would search your soul to think of anyone you have wronged and let us know. It is one thing to watch a video and another to pierce the soul for information."

"There will be 3 judges presiding over the case. Judge Wapner will be the lead judge for this case."

"Where have I heard that name before? I could recognize it."

"He was famous for the People's Court. You used to watch it with your grandma in Syracuse."

"Right, he was a fair person."

"Yes, he was and still is."

"Because you were an unexpected case, we will be starting your trial in three days."

"How long does it usually last?"

"Good question, it just depends. You are not a murderer, so it will not be a case decided in an hour. Usually, cases like yours take a while because you are a normal human who has flaws, but a lot of positives. God created humans to have flaws. Imagine a world of all perfect people."

"Ms. Jenkins, can you tell me about you?"

"My full name is Abigail Jenkins. I am originally from a small town near Houston. The way it works up here is that you are assigned judges and counsel from your country on Earth so that you or the client feel more comfortable. Anyway, I had three children and they are all young adults now. I worked for a nonprofit that helped the poor get counsel if needed. Fortunately, my husband's job paid a decent salary to allow me to work there. I enjoyed my job, met a lot of struggling families, and I was proud to serve them."

"Can I ask why you are here then?" Sounds as if you should be in heaven.

"Well, good question. My husband, who I love dearly was my second husband. However, he never knew that I never got divorced from the first. I was in an abusive relationship with my first husband. I was beaten, cursed, and spat at. I had broken ribs. Finally, I found a group that could help me. They got me out of the house and drove me to several places all over the United States. I would spend weeks at different locations to draw him off the scent. Ultimately, I was given a new identity. Given, but not legally. When I moved to Houston, I started taking community college courses. Over time, I earned my degrees and took the test to become a lawyer all under the alas. The judges admired that. The one thing they could not overlook was that I never told my husband about my past and that I was still married to Richard. The judges did not want to see me go to hell. They sentenced me here to work in purgatory and advocate for people to go to heaven. In two years, I hope to be able to walk out with my last client through those gates."

That is quite a background. It makes me wonder what the opposing counsel is like.

"Al Davis…right..well, for the most part, he is a good guy. You are lucky to have him as the opposing counsel. This is not to say that he won't give his best. He will, but he shows compassion. There are two types of opposing counsel. The ones that the devil employs to get the job done and the ones sentenced to work in purgatory. For example, I have been sentenced to 10 years to work cases as an advocate before I can go to heaven. The same applies to Mr. Davis. He was a huge corporate lawyer in Atlanta. He was very successful in defending his clients. However, in one particular case, he lost. His client had to pay millions of dollars to a class action suit. Mr. Davis went out drinking. Being a lightweight, meaning he does not normally drink, he decided to drink in front of an Amtrak train. The rest is history. When he went on trial up here, the judges saw a lot of good. He donated his time to build homes for Veterans. He fostered dogs, raised a moral family, and went to church every Sunday. They knew he lacked courage due to his last action on Earth, so the judges could not award him heaven. They also felt he did not deserve to go to hell, so they sentenced him to 10 years of service in purgatory. After ten years of stellar work, he may proceed to heaven."

"Does stellar mean his rate of wins?"

"No, it means that he did his best for the community."

"I'm confused….what about the deadly sins? I thought people were judged on those as well."

"Charles, can you name all seven deadly sins?"

"Ummm….There is….Sloth, gluttony, wrath, lust, and greed…..that five…."

"Can you think of examples of those…."

"Sloth, well a lot of people stay in jobs because they pay the bills or are just too lazy. Gluttony reminds me of Joey, on the show called "Friends" who wanted to eat everything; in one episode, he wanted to eat a Turkey all by himself. Wrath, you see it wherever people are honking their horns or screaming at another person. Greed is when people are being selfish or materialist. That can be seen among boys who want the latest Switch game to a person who is a hoarder."

"Charles, the other two are pride and envy."

"Well, those are common traits people have. Pride, knowing that you are very good at something. For example, I have a math teacher who prides herself on a 95% mastery rate. As for envy, I will use myself as an example. I envied people who stayed friends with a person I thought I was close to. Most people have some envy in them."

"Charles that is the point I am trying to make. Nine out of ten of my clients would go to hell if we followed the ten deadly sins. With so many different religions out there, it would not be fair to judge them on those. With Pope John Paul at the helm, God transitioned up here as well. He realized most people are good in nature. He believes the attributes I described will tell if a person deserves to go to heaven or not. Think to yourself, would you be able to go to heaven if we judged you on the seven deadly sins? You do an act once and you are in hell. That is why God created this trial system. God realized that these were common traits in people. It would be unfair to judge people on them, so he devised this concept that we follow. The judges are all people in heaven, but they still serve. For the most part, they get to be in heaven 90% of the day."

"I guess you don't say no to God."

"They could have because God permits them the choice. It is rare for someone to say no because they see the greater goal in mind and want what is best for the community. Alright, if you have no further questions, I will send you a message when and where we should meet. The message will come with a light on your arm. So much better than text messaging on phones. Most meetings will be near the judicial building. This building is designed similar to our Supreme Court building, just a lot larger. The columns are breathtaking and the scales of justice are perched right in front of the building."

"Sorry, I do have one. How many clients do you do at a time?"

"Chuck, only one. We put all of our energy into the one client we are working with. Even when a family perishes at once, they each get their own advocate. Have a great day and explore this beautiful area."

Explore

⌘

Later that day, after I had returned to my hotel room, I went onto the deck. The setting was the Hudson River. It was not from the Walkway, but from a room. I knew immediately that it was not the Hudson River that made this special, but the room that had the scene. It was from Vassar Hospital. When both my children were born, we had the same post-birth room. We requested it the second time as it brought luck to us the first time. Those were some of my happiest days. My wife was safe and healthy. My children brought tears to my eyes. The warmness of the visitors from diverse parts of my life came to visit and offer their blessings. We are a community that needs to stay together. Those moments definitely displayed that.

As I was just gazing out, I heard a knock on my door. I began to think who it might be. "Please God only good news." I got my robe on and it was one of my old friends who just passed away about a week ago. Due to COVID restrictions, I did not go to her wake even though my heart was there. She worked in my building and most of the time brought a smile to my face. She always had questions and opinions about what was going on. She also knew everything as she was the main office sectretaryto the school and her uncle was a member of the Board of Education.

"Chuck, how are you? I hope they are treating you alright here."

"They are, Sophia. I wanted to come to your wake….I just couldn't."

"I get it. I just hope Dave has not been off-colored since I left."

"Dave is a good guy; comments he has made came from his heart. I would not expect it any other way."

"How are the girls?"

"They are alright. When I last saw them, the little one was still being a monkey, jumping and climbing all over me. Her smile is infectious. The oldest thinks she is a teenager but wants to put a smile on all of her friends' faces. She is trying to create a zoom call to keep everyone connected."

"L is teaching from home. She misses going into her building though. Like all teachers, they want to teach kids, but also have a community atmosphere."

"Well, I am glad to hear it. I want to show you a few things. I know they have been busy up here, so your tour guide probably has not arrived yet."

As we stepped outside, we walked in a direction I have not been to yet. In the distance, I could see a great big billboard. As we moved closer, the old Grand Central Station flip board tells one what trains were about to depart and arrive. However, instead of trains, there were people. Instead of one billboard, there were several thousand by regions. The difference was that you can put your hand on the control panel and personalize one of the flip boards to see anyone who connected with you that is expected to pass away soon or when their trial is expected to be over.

"Chuck, I check this every day. You did not show up on my board until yesterday when it mentioned your trial. What happened?"

"Good question. It was normal if you want to call it a normal day. Well, you never experience our new normal. Our normal day consists of no kids in the building, no laughter, only tears. The building seems abandoned after dismissal which creates a very lonely environment. On my last day on Earth, an ex-husband came to see a teacher and was not happy we asked him to leave. So, he shot me. We called a lockdown, hopefully, it went smoothly and no one else was injured. Would I have known if anyone passed away?"

"Chuck, you were the only one that came up on the board. I think we were fortunate that kids were not in the building, I think we were fortunate that a lot of teachers were quarantined at home."

"Oh, you know about the quarantine that goes on?"

"In your room, your screen has a channel that allows you to watch what is going on with the people you care about. I have been keeping tabs on Dave, my uncle Ray, and my boys. I have been keeping tabs on the school and those parents are still interesting. I miss the friendly parents that would come in for their children, but I definitely do not miss the angry ones who think they are entitled. People do not realize how much time it takes for the tracing that you do. There are times I look at Kathy and say to myself, "Kathy, I will help you with that. Just let me do it for you." I know I can't, but I don't know how I can or who can help her. So, anyway, would you like to continue the tour?"

"Sure, that would be great."

"Sophia, what do you do for food? Not that I am hungry, but I miss eating."

"We do not need to eat, but your tour guide would tell you that anything you eat will not affect you, but can still satisfy you. We go to what is called Hickey Hall. I don't know how the name came about, maybe God is trying to be funny. Let's go and check it out. I can use a hot fudge sundae anyway."

"Isn't it early for that?"

"Time does not matter up here. If you want eggs, you will have eggs. You want Crème Brule, have fun. You sit down and order whatever you want and within minutes, it comes out. Hickey Hall has several rooms with different themes, so you can get the experience you want."

"Now that we are here, what theme do you want? Just please do not say a Chucky Cheese environment, or I will have to slap you."

When she asked me that question, my heart sank. L and I always would ask each other what we wanted to eat. It was a running joke, but yet not a joke as we could spend a long time deciding. It was always a mutual group decision, one that I really only want to make with her. I don't have her. I don't want to look on the screen either to see her as I might break down. Why is this only hitting me now? I think I have been so wrapped up with all the new things here that I didn't consider how my family was doing. I hope they know I am alright up here, at least for now. Who knows what will be in store after the trial.

"Chuck, I asked what you are in the mood for."

"Sorry, you decide, Sophia. I am game for anything, but seafood. Alright, I know what to choose."

"Sophia, how do you do it?"

"What's that?"

"You always had a brave face, even now. But don't you miss Dave and the boys? I think of Lisa and the girls quite a bit up here."

"I miss them a lot, but I need them to move on. I need Dave to do his plumbing job. I need the boys to look after their kids and provide their families with a good home. I am sure you want the same for Lisa."

"I do. Lisa was my rock. Whenever I needed someone to stand next to me, she did. I mean she would definitely tell me when I was wrong, but she stood by. Even when we were dating, I was her assistant principal while she was a teacher. Our principal knew and we kept everything open with the other APs. There was a guy who wanted my job and told people. However, he also made up stories or bluntly lied. She would come home and say "Hey, did you say this about so and so". I would look at her with an inquisitive look. The next day, she found an opportunity to call him out by saying, "Well if Chuck said that, we should all talk to him." He backed peddled so fast that he never lied about me again. She knew, after our third date, she told me we would get married. "You might be my boss now, but I will be your boss for the rest of our lives". Who knew my life would be this short?"

"Chuck, the only thing you get from looking back is a stiff neck. Yes, you should be able to grieve like them. First, you need to get into heaven. Now, let's get going to the table, so I can taste the food."

After our Mexican food capped with flan, I went back to the room to rest for the night. I think I will watch some of the 90s. I loved my high school years. I had a close-knit group of friends and loved my classes. I drove my Blazer which I absolutely loved. It was my baby. The Dean of Students would let us go to D&D or for pizza if we gave him a coffee or a slice. He was super cool, but to know everything I know now, it totally was not a safe move. I also looked back at New Year's Day throughout the 90s. I stayed by myself plenty of those times because I always felt I did not have friends. But now I realized I was asked each year to go to some party, but I always declined. Either it was a long drive or I was tired. In the end, I just made some excuses and missed out on good times. I looked at the parties and they looked like fun. I would have had a blast. I was told by people throughout the years that I am my own worst enemy. I can own it, but then give me the tools to overcome.

Sophia did offer to give me the rest of the tour, but I told her I will take small steps. I was actually missing my family quite a bit. One thing she did tell me was that the train I was puzzled about was called the downtown train. This is the train for the very few who return back to Earth. It was very rare and it means the judges needed to confer with the higher-ups for clarification and approval. Her tour guide explained that it has not happened for years. The Downtown train has almost been a piece of art and people are told upfront that they should not expect to the million-dollar winner to that ride home.

The next day I actually got my official tour; some places were to re-familiarize myself. However, he also showed me the recreation building, library, and the hall of fame. Russel, the tour guide explained that all of these buildings are heavily used. Some people like to go to the library to figure out any loopholes to get them into heaven. This library is old school, not like how our school library currently looks like. Our school library offers cozy nukes where students can relax. It offers a lot of Tec places and walls you can write on. This library is mandatorily silent. In there, the newspapers from Earth cannot be slanted. Instead, they have "Heaven Times" and you can look up anything you want. For example, since I am a history buff, I looked up dilemmas that were never truly solved or one people had conspiracies about. For example, Russia and the mobs had nothing to do with Kennedy being assassinated. Grant was drunk when Lee offered over his sword, and when the USS Maine went down, it was because of faulty machinery. We did get the election correct with Biden and Trump owes a lot of taxes. Bush handled 9/11 efficiently and Elvis is definitely dead. Russel did offer some advice. Try not to get too close to people in this realm. You may never see them again and your only focus should be on you. He was not saying we shouldn't be compassionate, but this can be a big win or loss. You need to do everything and anything to win since the advocates are swamped. So, you must get your hands dirty and remember things that can help you. For example, if you did anything with the mentally disabled, that can help if you did community service, or as simple as treating others with respect. Sometimes, the littlest of things can sway the vote. You don't need all three votes to go your way, you need just two. He suggested going to the park, order some food from one of the food trucks, and relax near the lake. He said there was a castle that overlooks the swans on the lake. Funny, how much these people know about me as he said the castle is a bigger version of the Belvedere Castle in Central Park. This was where Lisa and I got married. As I approached the Castle, I could see people playing baseball, soccer, and tag football on the fields. One of the soccer players actually looked like Diego Maradona. In his day, there was no one better. It looks like he still has his skills. No sense in getting autographs up here as I don't think they will likely go wherever I am headed. Hopefully, my daughters take care of my autograph collection at home. I never did get Nicole the Aaron Judge autograph she wanted. When she met him, she got only a wave and was told he doesn't give autographs at that event. Yet, he posed for pictures with the little boy right next to her. I wanted to make her happy. It wasn't going to happen though since I got rid of my Yankee season tickets after 15 years. The prices were unreal, especially during COVID. Then, after my family witnessed other teams cater to families, we realized the Yankees were not a family team. I never thought one of my daughters would root for the Orioles and the other the Phillies. However, both teams treated my kids like they were royalty. Even the Royals' players would say hi to my kids before a game. Then when you basically pay for a Yankee event and you get sidestep for a wave, you know your time buying season tickets is over.

I got a hot dog at a vendor and climbed the castle stairs. It reminded me of the Castle I slept in while in Dublin. It had armor all around, grand fireplaces, and tapestries of different clans. If they had clan McNab up there, I would be delighted. Suddenly, it appeared. God really does work wonders. Its motto said "Timor Omnis Asbestos," meaning "Let fear be far from all". Reflecting on that for a bit, my ancestors were right. You cannot let fear interfere with your life. The worry is usually 95% and the action is 5%. The worry is usually the worst part of the whole thing. It is like having an angry phone call by a parent at 3:59 on a Friday. You let it go to voicemail, but all weekend you worry about what was on the voicemail. Then on Monday, it will actually be the parent apologizing for how they acted.

I moved to the roof and take in the scenery. The flowers are in bloom and people were having a lot of fun tanning, reading books, or playing games. As I was up there, a person who seemed out of breath came dashing at me.

"Can you play? Our catcher just got summoned to the court-house and we need an extra player."

"Umm, I would love to, but my shoulder....I cannot throw a ball any longer after I tore it."

"Buddy, no one has injuries up here. Take this ball and throw it to that guy on the field."

"Really? I might hit someone and I can't control any throw anymore."

"Just do it. You will be fine."

Alright. Just like that, I threw it and it went right to him on two bounces. I was so excited. Not since 9th grade have I played a real game. That isn't entirely true. In 9th grade, I tore my shoulder. I still played the whole season before going to the doctor. He told me I could have surgery to repair it, but I would have to retear it first since it healed incorrectly on its own. My dad and I opted for physical therapy but it never truly worked. The next year, I played on travel ball. Played is a funny word as I basically warmed the bench. I remember trying to get into games, but I would get one at-bat during a game we were losing. To be that player, to be the washed up...it was time to hang up the cleats. It was the best decision I ever made though. I started to focus on my grades. I realized if I put my energy there I could amount to something useful in life. Now, though I get to play baseball pain-free. This brings me back to my childhood where my father built me a batting cage in our Peekskill back yard. I would spend hours honing my skills from both the right and left sides of the plate.

"Hey, I will be down there in 2 minutes. Is there a gear?"

"Ha, ha...we have all the gear you can possibly need or rather won't need since no one gets hurt."

I did alright with a double and a walk and no one ran on me. Thank you, Jesus. I called a decent game and we won by two runs. Afterwards, Shane invited me to go to the mall with him.

The Mall was a quick trolley ride from the park. Shane, who was the right fielder in the game, told me the mall had all the old stores that we had while growing up. Looking up at it, it resembled the Palisades Mall that I used to go to. Walking into it, it had the exposed piping, the concrete floors, but it also had the old mall maps which you do not see many of its kind in the dwindling malls scattered around the country today. Caldors, Filienes, Sears, and Jamesway were the anchor stores. Honestly, I don't know how you would have Caldors and Jamesway in the same area. It is like having a Walmart and Target in the same mall. Crazy Eddies was a techie store filled with televisions in its window displays. Why would anyone want to buy a TV here? I must not have thought that in my head and said it out loud. Shane quickly chimed in that it gives people a comforting feeling knowing they can see part of their past. No one here has money to buy anything. If you really want something, just ask and they will give it to you. You can think of it as a museum experience. Really, the only places I see people actually get things is from the Fotomat outside the mall. You ask the people there for certain pictures and they readily get them for you. For example, I use to love going trout fishing with my nephews. I asked them for a picture of it and they picked the moment that Davie caught a 7-pound trout. It was his first catch ever. We were so proud of him. I don't know why but I immediately thought of my DJing days at the Buzz. Currently, they are ranked number two nationally by the Princeton Review. My partner, Jess, and I had put a lot of work into our show and I wish I had a picture of when I was in college doing that. I wish I also had pictures of Madison saying mercy when I tickled her or Nicole showing off her terrific smile.

As we walked through the mall like Mallrats, we passed Service Merchandise, Radio Shack, Blockbuster, KB Toys, Sharper Image, Modells, Tower Records, Warner Brothers, Kinney Shoes, and even Walden Books. It also had a Filnese. My Lisa once worked there. That would have been great seeing her fold the new inventory, greet customers, and make change for a local shopper. I could see that warm smile generating sales for that department store. As we walked by that entrance, people were playing with remote control cars at KB. A clerk was showing off how to do turns in the air with a foam airplane as well. In the center of the hall was a person selling heat packs and another demonstrating how to use a steaming gadget. KB also had a display of the most frightening toys ever made such as the giraffe troll dolls and the Madball foam balls from the 1980s. Sharper Image had the chairs you can sit in for the massage and Walden books might as well be a library as all the tables were filled. It was awesome seeing Bugs Bunny welcome people into the Warner Brother Studio store and the other characters positioned just right throughout the store. I never quite understood how they did not survive and Disney did. The only thing I could think of was that at Disney, you are always treated as though you were a guest. Tower Records had the music blasting away to "Open Your Heart" by Madonna. The top ten list was there for everyone to see, but it wasn't from 2020, but from 1986. I asked Shane why it was so and he said that they usually changed it every hour. There was a food court that even had a Friendly's. This was like the Friendly's at the JV Mall where I met Captain Lou Albano. It had a walk-up window to place your order. While in senior year, and after school each day, my friend and I would stop at the mall to get a fribble. Then we would pass the Bourbon, Chinese, and Japanese restaurants to get the samples. After a while, you would think the people would stop giving us food, but they knew we meant no harm and we were always were polite. The one thing we saved our money for was for the pizza, like slices of cookies. How incredibly tasty those cookies were. In this mall, they had one right next to a movie theater. The theater is called Hoyts Cinema. Wow, it felt like a day at an amusement park reliving my childhood. By this time, Shane introduced me to other people that were on the same train with him to the afterlife. He was a really social person. I was getting tired and wanted to see what scenery awaited me on the deck. I wished him good luck and took a trolley back to the hotel.

When I got back, the lobby clerk had a message for me. I took the envelope up to my room, used my finger to open the message, and smiled with delight. Sophia had made it to heaven. She left me a note to encourage me to stay strong. As I walked into my room, I could see the image overlooking the deck. It was when I proposed to Lisa in Atlanta. It was her image with the backdrop of the view from the Sun Dial Restaurant. This was the highest restaurant in the northern hemisphere that rotated. It gave a skyline view of the entire city. I still remember us taking a taxi to the restaurant. The driver kept looking back to talk to us and Lisa was getting annoyed. She kept saying "let's go back and order Chinese." Later on, I found out that she knew somehow that I was proposing and wanted to have a little fun at my expense. It worked. I was so ticked off at her that when I finally tried to propose, I could not get the words out. She just said yes. Looking back at it, it was a funny situation if you were there. I forgot to mention that a fog appeared as we were eating. Fortunately, the restaurant allowed us to come back the next day to see the view. As I was sitting outside I noticed my wrist started to blink. It was a message from Ms. Jenkins. I needed to be at Chamber 102 promptly at 9:30. If you are late you might as well pack your bags to hell.

Channel of Lisa and School

❧

Before going to bed, I turned on the Current Channel. It allowed me to see what was going on in my life on Earth. There was a lot going on about Mr. West's situation. The aftermath was making National news headlines. CNN was covering with Dr. Gupta, explaining why a person can go mentally ill when obsessed with a loved one. He broke down Mr. West's life and the relationship he had with his ex-wife. CBS news kept calling me a hero. However, a lot of newspapers like the New York Times had questions.

The headlines from the different papers were:

NY Times – "Why wasn't the SRO at the scene?"

Poughkeepsie Journal – "District not getting full funding, could have prevented shooting"

NY Post – "SPOs furlough..really?"

Daily News – "Who is this hero?"

Their headlines went right to the point. If the state had not taken a 20% cut in district funding, things might be a little bit easier on districts, especially when we are in the hole by millions of dollars and we are not even halfway through the year. Cuomo is a democrat but has never really cared for schools like his dad. Our superintendent needed to cut, especially if kids were not in the buildings. For all the talk that our superintendent is like Dark Vader, he does have a heart. He did not furlough the 100s of employees that were bus drivers, monitors, and bus monitors even though that would have saved the district a lot of money.

The questions that the papers should be asking are, "How did he slip into the building?" and "Why is the Auditorium door in the mantrap?" It allows penetration from unwelcomed guests.

One channel was interviewing Lauren about how she handled the situation when she became incident commander. That is the verbiage for a person in charge during a crisis. She explained that the district office and police were called when I signaled Kathy. The teachers were placed in lockdown and when the Sheriffs came they checked every room to ensure that there were no other perps. As the Sheriffs, MTA police, State Troopers, and local police went into every room, they told everyone to leave everything inside the room except for valuables. As the rooms were checked, they took large black sharpies and wrote on each door. Police were lined throughout the hallways to ensure that the students did not see where the shooting had occurred. Then the pupils were shepherded out of the building like sheep onto buses to a reunification site.

The reporter asked her how she coped with this as a second-year AP and she said it was not something they train them in school for and that it was just a dark day for us all. I expected better vocabulary from her as she was a wizard for finding unique words, but I guess she must have been exhausted. At least she didn't use any four-letter words that would normally also pop out of her mouth.

Lauren told the reporter she had to go as the superintendent needed her and ended the interview. Once her superintendent arrived, Lauren handed over the incident command to him. The superintendent informed Lauren that our staff was to stay in our building and that the other four buildings would assist the kids during the reunification. Any staff that was on the busses would return to our building but would enter through the football field gate since the main lobby was a crime scene. I was thinking our safety plans were fully intact. Our reunification plan which consisted of the other buildings partnering up was working.

As the police were handling their business, Lauren called an emergency faculty meeting. Any available counselors and clinicians that were not at the reunification site were in separate rooms in our building to help anyone in need. I did not recognize any of the clinicians, but their ID badges were an array of colors. Looking closer, they were from a neighboring school district. Our enemies on the sports fields were our companions in crisis. After the faculty meeting, she checked on some monitors that were close to Chuck.

What was really sad was that the last child did not leave our building until roughly six hours later, to be reunited with his family. Lockdowns are a scary place. We as a nation need to change our ways to control anger, to heal social emotion issues so our kids do not get hurt in the process. When students, staff, or members of our community think they can walk into a school and open fire, then we are failing our kids. The other option would be using metal detectors, but what type of atmosphere is that?

I wanted to see how my students were doing. The channel shifted to students staring out from the buses to a flood of police lights that resembled a Newark runway at night. Once the students got to the reunification site, they signed in, showed their IDs, and were ushered into a large room. There they sat by homeroom. Kids looked confused while strangers sat them down. Most of the people checking the kids in were district office officials. You could see the elementary principals rotating through the rooms while teachers are running kids to a separate hallway to connect with their parents. At least with this lockdown, no child would be missing. No parent would cry tears of sadness, but tears of joy. Students were given pizza and most just stayed silent. The ones that were crying were escorted to small rooms filled with clinicians. As it got late, people went to the remaining students to ensure a parent was picking them up and asked to call emergency contacts if needed.

The last time a family member was really sick was my mom who had quadruple heart surgery. Since it was during COVID, only my father was allowed to go to both hospitals that she was at. We told the girls she was at a hospital having minor surgery to feel better. We made sure to be gentle so our 5-year-old won't understand since our oldest child freaks out about everything. When my mom was out of the hospital and recovering, we started to FaceTime her a lot, and one day my oldest child noticed a big scar on the top of my mother's chest. She asked her what it was and she responded that it was where they needed to open her up to heal her. My oldest realized there was more to the story than we had originally told her. The other time we had an issue was when my mother-in-law was ill. We just told the girls she was on a vacation to be by herself. Lisa told the girls I was on a business trip. They know once in a blue moon I am on work-related conferences. I really hope they don't get fruit baskets or cards because they all normally send cards when someone is ill. My girls love opening up cards. Lisa better watch out. Lisa also kept the TV on to only DVR of the girls' shows or Netflix. Such a smart idea. She lets them watch Mickey's Clubhouse or Fuller House. She knew that doing so was better than getting five seconds of the news. If somehow the girls find out that I was at the hospital, for example, a teacher accidentally says something, Lisa will tell the girls I had a small accident. However, because of COVID, they cannot come to see me. They will believe that because we were not able to talk with mom. I also saw Lisa writing an email to the principal and teacher at their school to not discuss the matter with them. Let's hope no one randomly does so. If I was there, I would have debated the tactic, but that's the problem…I am not there.

Lisa started to cry as she left the girls watching Fuller House. She headed to the bathroom and she burst into tears while praying. She wasn't the praying type. Lisa is a very secure person who always said the only thing you get for looking back is a stiff neck. I know this is different. In her prayers, she was offering things to God if I survived.

I love her so much. She is the ultimate package. I wish she would think of some of our happier moments to get her through this ordeal. She always challenged me to do my best, never walked away from a fight, but always found the resources to overcome; that is what I need right now next to my side. I need my L to be my support. Yeah, I might be a successful administrator and well respected, but it wasn't just me who got me here. She helped mold me into the administrator and the person I became. I never wanted her in my shadows. Sometimes she would say to me, "You know if I had focused as much as you on continuing my education, I would be right with you." I do think she was wrong with that sentiment as she probably would be superintendent now. She reminds me of the combination of presidents' wives. From Nancy Reagan's savviness and ambition to protect her husband from jerks to Eleanor who had no problem sharing her opinion with FDR, even if he didn't want to hear it. It is funny though because he realized that she was right most of the time. Laura Bush was the anchor that kept the family and George Bush on the right track, and my wife certainly does that as well. She needs to put all those traits that I know she has and help our girls out. She will turn into Edith Wilson, who after Woodrow had a stroke and became the gatekeeper. I can see if that lean chance of survival occurs, she would probably make any person take an entrance exam to see me. However, there is a slim chance she will get that opportunity as I am on trial to determine if I am going to hell or heaven. Thank goodness she has her parents next door to help her right now. I am sorry that I put her in this position.

She fell into my lap when I wasn't paying attention like the psychic had told me. When I first met her, the psychic said I should leave my current girlfriend outside as we wouldn't be dating for much longer. Joanne then preceded to say I would meet her at work, but it was during the third time that we had an opportunity to work together that everything clicked. Well, in New Hyde Park, I was hired to teach on the same team as Lisa, but she took a new job in Croton. The following year, I went to Croton and was offered either to work in the middle school or high school. I chose the high school. If I had picked the middle school, L and I would have been on the same team again. We finally met when I became the AP at the middle school and the rest was history. Some parts of the story vary, depending on who you ask. She will say that I asked for her personal email so I could start talking to her, but the reality is, I asked everyone for their personal email to ensure I had a way to contact them if an emergency happened at night. She was right though. When we started emailing each other, I would send her corny jokes because she was a goddess and totally not in my league. Rather, I was not in her league. She finally told me to stop sending her forwards and jokes. She concluded that statement by asking me out. Naturally, I accepted. As we started to date, we realized that we could not be in the public eye. We would go a weekend trips all over the North East. When it started to get serious, we told the other admin in the building so that we could keep our relationship transparent. It was funny because the principal at the time reminded Lisa that he is the reason we started to date. I was inquisitive about how that was possible. Then he said that while she was chaperoning at the last school dance, he went over to her and suggested that I was an eligible bachelor and she should grab me if she had the chance. I don't know how I did not laugh, but more power to him if he got the idea in her head because that eventually blossomed into my beautiful family. It was my principal though who changed the course of Lisa and my life forever. L and I were already engaged, but she wouldn't wear the ring at school because too many questions would be asked. He came to my office to ask how Boston was and I told him that the car attendant drove our car on wet paint in the parking lot, but besides that, it was very romantic. He then asked what was Lisa's favorite part of the trip. As he said it, one of the biggest gossipers on the building came from behind and said "Lisa who?" Without thinking, he said, "You know Lisa blah blah". Yup, that was the end of the secret. By the end of the day, everyone in the building knew. In the weeks that followed, the district office said one of us would have to transfer to another building in the school. The superintendent promised that if I found a new job, Lisa could stay at the middle school, otherwise, she would be transferred to the high school. A couple of months later after she was transferred, I got a better job in a nearby district, and Lisa told me that they offered her back the old job, but she loved the high school. To this day, L still loves the high school and I became well respected in my current district. It is amazing how one small slip-up could change your destiny. There was nothing going to stop Lisa and I.

She swore it would never end, but my actions caused it to end. I felt so awful about putting her into a situation where she felt she could only let out her emotion in the bathroom. I just wanted to be able to hug her. She was upset that her last encounter with me was arguing over putting the dishes into the dishwasher before the sitter came to watch the girls, as they were scheduled for a remote day for school. That isn't how our last moment should have been. This new normal makes people tensed over little things, Lisa and I included. The Counting Crows song "Rain King" started to play in my head. I remembered, but always knew, she was my queen.

Her parents were our next-door neighbors. They would check on the family several times a day. My brother drove up from Florida to be with my parents and help Lisa with the girls. Lisa focused on the girls and work to get her through the grief. She became, but always was the unheralded leader who could appear strong. She would always cry herself to sleep whenever she was alone, for example, when she is putting cream on Sophia's hands. I used to love telling her that her hands resembled the hand from Sophia on Golden Girls. I love you L.

On the channel, I also witnessed The Sheriff's investigation. I guess that is standard procedure when there is a weapon involved and/or a possible murder. What am I saying? I am up here, so it is murder even though they have me on life support down in the hospital. If they only knew to take me off the ventilator. Deputy Hunter was also investigated. They needed to go step by step with him. Was this a usual occurrence that Mr. West came to the school? Was he considered a threat in the past? Has he ever disobeyed the court order of protection? All these questions all popped up in my head. They went through a timeline of events with Tom. They even questioned him and Kathy if he had told me he was leaving for the other school. Everything turned out kosher, as he is a person who usually follows the book word by word.

As I was watching Tom at his office in the school, he was still engulfed with his books. He made sure he gets his reports done on time. However, he likes to have fun. He loves to play pranks and I will miss that. He once tried to get a balloon to pop hole punches when I opened my office. It failed miserably, but he tried. Once, I sent him a box from a guy in Pennsylvania that listed the contents as herpes medicine. He had to sign for it. The post office personnel was snickering when Tom signed for the box. He doesn't ever want to get outdone and he stated there are rules for pranks.

1. It cannot be a prank that gets the boss
2. Cannot use glitter. That can mess with someone really bad.

Tom is also someone really good to sound things off on. He is a great listener. You just have to watch if he starts talking and roping you back into his office when you need to do something else. He is a great person, friend, and police officer. He didn't need this on his watch. Thomas is also getting married soon. Cheers to both of them. He needs to get out of this funk he is in right now, stop his grieving, and relax he has some special things in his life. I wish there was a way I could get him to stop watching the video on me getting shot both times. He seems to have gone through step by step over a hundred times. It was just bad timing. He should be more impressed with my actions since I did not have my metal Michele Smith bat in my hands.

Finally, the yellow tape was removed at the school. No one was allowed in the building until the investigation was concluded. Not even the custodians. However, with the tape being removed from the lobby and the stairwell, the custodians were able to clean the blood. They went to different closets and started to pull out the buckets, mops, cleaners, and rags. Blood was puddled in the lobby and dripped in line through the hallway to the stairs. From there, blood flowed down the stairs with blood splattered over the wall as an outline of Mr. West. I heard one custodian say he would rather mop the throw-up in the cafeteria than this. Another claimed he would rather clean up the smears of feces on the walls in the bathroom that a girl did than clean this up. That girl was obsessed with a teacher and would write her name in it.

There was so much I ended up watching on the TV about what took place after the shooting. My superintendent put out a few robocalls. The first was to let the community know that there was a shooting at my school and that it would be close until further notice. He did not mention my name as they wanted to talk to Lisa first. He did say that someone was injured and that they should keep that person in their thoughts. Can't say a prayer as that is a political no-no. The second one was that the school would be reopened just for staff. We would continue to teach the students virtually as the county had one of the highest rates of COVID in the state. He ended both messages by saying that the community members should give their children extra hugs and be present in the moment with them.

Last year, I was able to get a gazebo built through a grant. It allowed people to have a shelter during the hot and rainy days while practice was going on in the upper fields. Well, one of Family and Consumer Teacher started an area next to the gazebo for teachers, children and community members to put flowers and lights. There were some lovely notes wishing me a smooth recovery. It is funny that the superintendent didn't think people knew, but everyone talks. The coolest letter was from one of my 7th graders who said, "Mr. McNab, you can put me in Lunch Detention for the rest of the year if it means you are back. You understand me and my craziness. No one else gets me as you do." That definitely warmed my heart. The custodians could hear singing till 11 pm that night. The songs were beautiful with Christian theme songs blasting throughout the field. I hate to say it, but they need to practice better social distancing or they might get COVID. Some of the teachers even talked about creating a bonfire, just as we would normally do for homecoming. Wow, this really influenced the community. I always said we were family, I am glad they believed that as well.

During this time, Mrs. West asked for a leave of absence. I don't blame her. She doesn't deserve all of this. Some people in the community were blaming her. How is it her fault? She was in the middle of a divorce. She had a restraining order. This should have been a safe zone. She took her kids and flew to her family in Colorado. I wouldn't be surprised if she relocated there. After all, our district is very good at giving leave of absence even if a person takes on a new position in another district. She did write a card to Lisa, expressing that her only sorrow was the tragedy that took place. She was one of the hundreds of cards in the mail from teachers and past and present students from every district Chuck worked at. There were also letters from people around the country saying how I was a hero and they need more people like me in the schools. You know what? You do have a lot of people like me in the schools. Unfortunately, it happened in my building. We love our kids and most staff would do what is needed to protect them. One of my former bosses jumped a fence and ran in the snow for miles, going over a log that ran across a stream to catch up to a student. He ended up going over 4 miles before he caught up to her. The police were happy because he ruined her tracks in the process and they couldn't use their dogs, but at the end of the day, she was found. The neighboring districts were offering social workers and school psychologists to help with counseling for the staff and students. You can see how communities come together during a crisis. North Salem might be a rival on the field, but a brother when we need them.

The last thing I saw before I went to bed was that Lisa did something with the girls that made me gush like the Victoria Falls. The girls and I loved turning my Ipad on and playing the music on the gadget. Actually, they would even fight on which song would be played. Tonight, Lisa put on Darius Rucker and Luke Bryan songs and they all danced like it was one of the first seasons of Grey's Anatomy. They just danced and danced until they fell asleep on the couch. I stared at that for them for quite a while until Lisa started wrestling with a throw pillow. She woke up, placed blankets on the girls, and went to our bed. She didn't sleep immediately, instead, she put a set of headphones on and listened to Fleetwood Mac. When she plays Fleetwood or the Indigo Girls, I know she is searching for answers. She then started to sing in a soft voice the lyrics of "Everywhere".

She drifted to sleep in an upright manner on the bed as she was singing. Lisa, I can hear you calling. I wish I never put you in this situation. You are a fantastic mother and wife. You will survive. I only wish I gave you more. I wish I also listened to Ken about life insurance.

Day 1 of the Trial

I went through the motions of walking into my shower, pressing the buttons, and moments later, I was in my suit. It was my lucky Michael Kors dark blue suit and I would wear it at important events like accepting the award from Putnam County for my Suicide Prevention campaign. Before I left my room, I looked into the mirror. Funny, on important days I would look into the mirror and talk to myself, give myself a pep talk of sorts, and today would not be any different. "Chuck, you have been a caring person who wanted what was best for you, your family, and your community. People might say differently, but you have to believe in yourself. You are the walking proof that good exists in the world." With that, I checked to see if my tie is too long and straighten it out at my collar.

It was yet another beautiful day outside as I walked to the Judicial building. Birds were chirping, squirrels chasing each other along the walk, I even noticed choco, the black squirrel from college eating a nut. It felt like Mayberry as people said hello as they walked by. This was so different than the NYC-like rush I felt the first day I arrived. As I arrived in the Judicial building, there was a water fountain piercing out of the angel's mouth. Giant marble steps direct you to the entrance, and as you enter, the grand building has pictures on every wall. The directory on the side helped me located Chambers 102. I have never seen a chamber looking so stunning. Normally, I was used to either the chambers you see on TV or the county chambers that was extremely sterile. This had paintings covering every speck of space from different eras and regions. With that being said, the advocate and I sat at a table in the center of the circular room.

The judges were seated in a pyramid shape high on the northern wall. There was a small viewing gallery on the southern wall like in a second-tier section of an old movie theater. Finally, the prosecutor sat at a desk at the eastern wall. However, when it was his turn to talk, I guess he liked to walk around. Ms. Jenkins said, "The judge's offices were behind their desk on the opposite side of the wall." Ms. Jenkins claimed that she once had to go to Judge Taft's office. It was large and elegant with statues everywhere. He also had a replica of a tub from the White House. That is funny.

The court officer started the hearing and the judges came in and introduced themselves. Judge Wapner was the lead judge with Judge Taft and Judge Ginsburg on either side. Judge Ginsburg just recently passed, probably the reason why she was not leading her own chamber. She was the "equity" movement before anyone ever realized there was such a thing. She started out in law when women were portrayed as housewives, where her intelligence was never questioned, but her gender was. She realized while developing a course at Rutgers that there were very few cases that dealt with women's rights. At the same time, the ACLU were getting complaints like, "how does a male worker get insurance for his family, but not a female worker?" Judge Ginsberg, as an attorney, went on to represent the ACLU on a number of cases and won. Afterwards, she was a champion of all people who were not treated equal. If she had the power, the Equal Rights Amendment would have been passed. I was curious why Judge Taft, who used to be a president, did not lead his own chamber. But that is God's decision. He was the first and only president to hold both offices and was known as a progressive president. Once a strong ally with Teddy Roosevelt, they soon became the worst of enemies. Taft is like me in many aspects. We were both cheery, had a distinct laugh, and many friends. However, he had very few closemates, and when one major friendship broke, he went into depression. It was said he went into depression when Teddy announced he was running against Taft. The depression not so much because of the competition, but it broke his heart. When I got like this, I was pretty closed off to the world. Cover my office window and just do work. In the same aspect, he did the same thing. History sees him as just an average president who got work done and went from 220 pounds to 300 plus, which supposedly caused him to get stuck in the tub. I probably should not ask him that.

Like I was told, the hearing starts with turning points. Turning points are moments that my life could have been altered based on the decisions I made. A huge movie screen appears on the left wall and a collection of the top 4 turning points were about to be displayed. The first one started with my mother asking me if I wanted to learn more about her culture and possibly some of the languages she knew. I told her no at the time because I was an outcast at school due to how I looked. I was the only tan boy in a school filled with black and white students. I tried to lean on my father's Scottish heritage, but that didn't get me far as people thought I either was lying or was adopted by him. However, at this turning point, I said yes and that I wanted to learn Swahili. As an elementary student, learning another language put me into a different realm that I never knew. As the years passed by, I craved the Saturday and Sunday Indian channels. Every Friday that we went to Indian House, I would speak to them in Swahili. I took the dance classes in New Jersey as a teenager and was noticed by some scouts who got me a deal to go to India and be an extra in some Bolly hits. After years of getting decent pay, I came back home to start my own dance studio in New York where Lisa was a client. We had two girls and then roughly in 2010, I was asked to join the crew of Just Dance. I would choreograph dance moves for the game. The turning point ended this year so I wouldn't know how much longer I would have had on Earth. The next turning point was when I dislocated my shoulder. I was stubborn and played the rest of the season and then realized I couldn't play baseball any longer. Still, this was different. I started the season as a backup catcher. My coach offered me techniques to throw the ball without putting pressure on certain parts of my body. I used to throw from my knees just like the great Benny Santiago. Gradually, I became the starter and had to work out to increase my strength. I ended up getting a scholarship for baseball at Siena College. I hit for contact but wasn't much of a homerun hitting. However, my switch-hitting capabilities interested MLB scouts. As a catcher, I also stole more bases than normal. In my senior year, I was voted MVP of the team and I was drafted in the 3rd round by the Blue Jays. It wasn't the Yankees, but I was happy. I used to love going to the Skydome with my relatives when I was young. After four years in minors and the last one in Buffalo, I was promoted to the majors when they were able to extend the rosters at the end of the season. My first at-bat came against Randy Johnson. He threw a pitch behind me as a welcome to the major's kid. I promptly struck out. Later, I walked and got my first hit down the middle. I spent the next two years going back and forth until my 4th year, where I got the nod in spring training that I would be a starter. I spent the next 11 years in the majors. I had a respectable 275 average. Then I spent the last 4 years as Andy Pettite's personal catcher. Whether he was with the Astros or the Yankees, wherever he went, I going as well. After I retired from baseball, I used the teaching certification that I gained at Siena and got a job at Croton school district. Caitlin Cathin, the cat, was principal at the time. She was amazed that she hired a former MLB player for PE and has a literature specialist certification. After a couple of years, I started to date a 7th grade math teacher. Again, Lisa and I lived happily with our two daughters. The next turning point was going to SUNY Albany. My dream after baseball was to go into politics. However, like a river, things can split or diverge. My first college choice was to go to SUNY Albany and I got accepted. I was going to study political science in the JFK building which was well-known. However, I ended up choosing St. Bonaventure because of the full scholarship. The video showed that if I had gone to Albany, I would have followed my dreams of being a politician. First, I would have had a 3.9 GPA for the 4 years. From there I would get accepted into Harvard Law. After successfully completing my law degree and passing the test, I would become a political lobbyist. Wow, this version of my life sounded quite different than what actually took place. I would join Governor Pataki's staff, While working for him in 2000, I was asked to do an assembly for the students at Buckner Middle School in New Hyde Park. At that time, I met a teacher I fell madly in love with. She would help me witness my political dreams come true by representing parts of Dutchess in the state legislature then ask the House of Representatives in District 18. We would have two beautiful girls. In 2020, I was debating on not to run for Governor and again, I cannot see what happen past this point. The last turning point that the movie reel showed was me getting a promotion. It showed my present life until 2018. Then I interviewed at a small district across the river. It was an hour commute, but it allowed me to be the Director of Instruction and Curriculum. It was a great job, but I started to have a lot of late nights and started to miss important events for the family. The worst was me missing my daughter's birthday. Lisa and I then separated, and it just got worst from there. In 2020 we tried to reconnect, but I could not see how things became to be. Judge Taft said three out of the 4 were good options that could have happened. I think I am just grateful that I went the route I did.

After the turning points that could have affected my life, Judge Wapner said that it is custom to show a highlight reel of what did happen. Ms. Jenkins said this could be a good indicator of what might happen as the verdict. However, it is not set-in-stone. It started with my mom racing down the city blocks with my dad to get to the hospital. You can see her asking to take a taxi and my father said they should walk it out because that will help with the delivery. It goes to the snowball fights I had with my dad behind the brownstone steps and how he used to let me sit on his lap and pretend to drive the car. From there it showed how I spilled a pot of coffee over my chest. The hours and days that my father sat by my side had the doctors dealing with the melting skin and skin grafts. The next year, I climber over the toilet to reach for something on the very top shelf and everything broke including the toilet, which pierced my foot. The last city picture was the constant super high fevers where the doctors put me in a tub filled with ice. At the time, they thought it was allergies. Wait, they had one more city event of me being carried by my dad as the girls on the street would say how adorable I was. The movie transitioned to Peekskill. Little league where I hit a homerun, this kid Daryl stealing my transformer (I wish Mrs. Smith could see this footage, now she would believe me), and how I felt like an outcast. However, it also showed how I worked at a day camp and the priceless memories, how I wrote poems and got two published, and finally had my operation that positively impacted my life. The movie displayed some of our family vacations including fly fishing in Canada and catching a 60 pounder…..my brother. My dad getting us safely off of a one-lane cliff road in Nova Scotia or the family being chased by a moose in Maine because I decided to pet the baby moose. Some of my favorite memories was sitting in the back seat of the car and drawing baseball card designs with my brother. Those were pretty special. When I was in college, it showed how I played Magic the Gathering, how when I got drunk, I would run throughout my dorm saying "I need air" and my friends would make sure the RAs wouldn't find me, and how I truly enjoyed my classes. It also showed the group study sessions at Perkins with the refillable hot chocolates, being a DJ at the Buzz, and playing ultimate Frisbee. During those summers, I would work in the Walmart photo lab. Probably one of my favorite jobs ever. I worked with a great crew, each with their own personality, but making something so beautiful out of chemicals and paper was awesome. Before my work career started, I went to the Buffalo Teachers Fair and was offered three jobs. One of them was Hyde Park. Teachers just did chalk and talk or dittos. I actually paid for a PowerPoint projector to give my kids a new experience. I loved giving kids experiences. However, the next experience was not so fun as 9/11 happened. In the video, I had to tell a boy that I am sure his birthday party tonight would be fun. Later in the year, I gave my students another experience with an overnight trip to Gettysburg. It was a smashing success until two kids hit their heads while playing a game in the recreational room during dinner. I was told by my AP that I had to stay up with them throughout the night to make sure nothing bad happened. Also, I came to find out that the rest of the teachers including the AP went out drinking. I called the principal the next day in tears. The rest of the year, I realized there was a cliché that I was not part of. The following year, I moved to Croton, more specifically John Jay High School. I felt part of that team of social studies teachers. I taught US History and Government. During this time, I took vacations that helped me become stronger in my field. I backpacked Egypt. Like the pyramids, rode a camel, slept in a sandstorm in the White Desert while foxes roamed over our sleeping quarters. I went to different European countries, including sleeping in a castle in Ireland, road tripping in Scotland, witnessing the four arms of Lake Lucerne and climbing the Eiffel Tower in France. In France, I rode a train going over 140 mph from Parish to Perpignan. I also skydived, piloted a plane over Sherwood Forest where I got to see the Major Oak from above, and went in a submarine in the Red Sea. However, one of my most prized encounters was working at Anderson; a school for Autistic students. I had 18 years olds on a first-grade level that summer. I had a lot of black and blues, but I realized that each child given an individual way to learn can prosper. When I became an AP at Van Wyck, life took an adventurous turn, I meant my future wife. We traveled to California, New Orleans, Chicago, and Europe. There, we went to the Biergarten in Munich, Museu Picasso where we saw over 4,000 pieces of work including the First Communion and the Alps of Austria. I proposed at the Sun Dial restaurant which is the highest rotating restaurant in the northern hemisphere. Soon, Lisa and I were given a choice. If I could find a new job, Lisa could go back to middle school instead of being transferred to high school. I found my new home in Todd Jr./Sr. High School. However, Lisa loved where she was at Jay and decided to stay there. For the most part, I have had great administrators to work with here minus one really lazy one who knows how to brown-nose while delegating her work to others. All in all, I had two terrific girls with my fabulous wife. The movie ends with the pandemic and then the shooting.

I thought the movie was condensed. They left out how I tried out for Jeopardy. Anyway, Judge Wapner explained that we would start with courage. He asked which side would like to go first. I guess there is no set order since there are only loose guidelines.

Courage

I t is no doubt that Chuck has courage. He has gone skydiving was his 21st birthday, backpacked Egypt after there was a hotel that was bombed, and when stranded at the side of the Nile because they wouldn't pay a ransom, he and his cousin figured out a way to get home safely. That way enlisted a convoy of Egyptian soldiers in an armored car. How is that not courage? We could also state that he was in a race car in Las Vegas and piloted a plane over the Sherwood Forest. However, he has demonstrated courage in other ways. At the Yankee playoff game, Cal Ripken was announcing the game from centerfield, Chuck climbed and hung on the rafters to ask Ripken for his autograph. Mr. Ripken even commented that he hung on there for a long time and wondered if it was worth his autograph. As for his career, he has had hard conversations with some staff. Had to tell a teacher that he did not feel comfortable having her in the classroom any longer, fired another staff member who was a parent for videotaping students in the hallways, and had to tell his boss that his boss made a serious mistake about a student. Lastly, he stood by his 2-year-old when she was in pain from her surgery, singing to her all night. Your honor, currently, I do not believe we need to call any witnesses as these facts demonstrate the courage of a fine person.

Mr. Davis then presented, "Your honors, in some ways, every-thing Ms. Jenkins stated shows either courage or darism. Does it take courage to find a way home from being stranded? Really, the other option would have been to sit at the Nile and hope nothing bad happens. At that point, he had to join the convoy or again sit there and hope nothing goes bad. Skydive is darism...he put himself in that position. The other act was that he was doing his job or his job would have been on the line. Finally, what parent would not comfort their child…I think if I am supporting the advocate, it is more of compassion than courage. Sorry, I forgot that he only went to Egypt after the bombing because his money would not get refunded."

"Charles, would you like to speak about these?"

"I think courage represents itself in many ways, your honors. Going to the Yankee Parade when I was 17 while supervising my younger brother? That takes courage because my parents were entrusting me to thinking safely for both of us. Skydiving and piloting showed how I was willing to step out of my comfort zone and take risks. In Egypt, trusting that the convoy would protect me instead of harming me takes courage and not backing down to a crook takes courage. I could have easily paid the ransom, after all, I was on his boat. I stayed cool and did not let the guy know that I did not like to swim. He really could have taken advantage of me. I just stood up for justice and what was right. Mr. Davis is right. I went to Egypt because the airline would not refund me my money. However, they did offer a voucher. Furthermore, my cousin was going regardless and I was going to join her. Courage is also about compassion."

A stone-faced Mr. Davis responded "Your honors, I have a few examples of Charles not having courage. May I proceed?"

"Go ahead Mr. Davis," stated Judge Taft

"We talked about him having the courage to have hard conversations, but he did not get rid of the unfit teachers in his building. There was a teacher who would stay home sick but would never call out. She would have her teaching assistant teach the class and her job was not terminated. Another teacher sat at the desk and told the students to use their text and notes to learn. Parents have seen this virtually, but she was not removed to get a better teacher. This shows a lack of courage. Let's continue to talk about jobs. There have been once-in-a-lifetime jobs that Charles should have gone for, but he didn't because it would affect his family. Is that courage? Why is Charles still an Assistant Principal all these years? He has gone for jobs and has been shortlisted several times. Does he sabotage himself because of his security blanket? He truly believes he has a family at his school, however, what he fails to understand is that everyone there is moving on without him. Sure, they shed some tears, after all, he spent 12 years with them. However, Dino is looking for a sub right now, interviewing them, joking, giving hugs, and telling some that he can see them fitting in quite nicely. That really sounds like a family to me, Mr. McNab. In fact, one candidate is discussing cuts of meat with Dino and was offered a second round on the spot. Look at that security blanket. Instead of progressing, he always had a reason why he did not get the job. He should look inwards and notice he just did not have the courage.

Finally, let's discuss his high school days. He was too shy in high school to ever ask the girl he had a crush on for a date. He would write her poems, slip them into her locker, but that was the closest he got for two years to express how he felt. I must admit that he finally had the courage three weeks prior to the junior formal dance, but when he asked her out, she said she was waiting because David Ducker asked her the night before. She was hoping he would build up the nerves, but at the same time, she wondered why he did not have the resolve to ask. In the English class, Danillia gave hints of the long bus ride homes, asking for help when she clearly did not need it. She even came to his locker to say she forgot often to write down the homework assignment for theology. Charles, just couldn't get out of his own way. I see someone who did not want to take the risk when those risks could have made him a better person. Thank you, your honors."

"Mr. Davis, I don't think you truly see what those examples represent about my client. Let's start with the most idiotic example. So, he didn't ask the girl he had a crush on. We all know from his records that even when he was 150 and thin as a rail, he thought of himself as a fat, ugly person. All the torment he had in elementary school about his weight truly affected him. That has nothing to do with courage, but rather hurtful words that affected him. Any job he did not apply for was because of family. He puts family first before anything else. Yes, he could have gotten the job across the river, but we saw in his turning point video what would have happened. He made the right choice. Mr. Davis, I would say if you cared about family, it would take courage to turn down that job. Lastly, on Earth, they have unions in schools. As an administrator, you must follow contracts. Those teachers I have observed have informal and formal conversations with reps, counseled them, got them mentors, and for one I even put the person on a teacher improvement plan. Yes, I wish as a group of administrators we need more, but I have set it in motion to either improve the teachers in question or find a way to part."

"Ms. Jenkins that was great. Can we call my grandpa to the stand? He can talk about when I was hit by the 18-wheeler and when I had a new engine in my Blazer."

"You think that will add to courage?"

"I think so…"

"Judge Wapner, would you allow us to present a witness at this time for courage?"

"Ms. Jenkins, I will permit the witness as long as it was a person already named."

"It was…counsel had this name from the beginning."

"We would like to call James McNab."

Mr. McNab, how do you know my client?

He is my grandson.

Have you witnessed him have courage?

My boy fought his way to earn the grades to make him successful. He taught kids and tried new things like fixing his electricity when he was inexperienced. He taught himself by asking questions to his father and checking YouTube. However, he is a determined s.o.b. as well.

"What do you mean?"

"It takes courage to get back on the road after he was hit by an 18-wheeler on the Thruway. It takes courage to survive an accident like that. It takes courage to deal with an officer who believed there was a domestic dispute instead of looking at the whole picture. It takes courage to deal with that officer after finding out the officer hates your Uncle who is also an officer."

"Can you tell us a little bit more about what happened?"

"He was hit from behind by the Penske truck. We presume the person was asleep at the wheel. By the time the officer arrived and realized it was a dispute, both Chuck and the girl were consoling each other. They tried to stop every Penske truck, but they realized it had gotten away. He would not drive for a few weeks until his father and I ordered him behind the wheel. We took it slow at first but Chuck gained confidence again."

"I-90, the Thruway that connects Greece to Syracuse has not been the friendliest to Chuck. At one point, his engine died. His Aunt picked him up and drove him to my house. His Blazer stayed at her house until we could find a place to fix it. There was a junk-yard near his college. They quoted him a price for an engine that had 110,000 miles on it and we agreed to the deal. However, when they said we should come, he was really sick, but he was determined. He stayed over at his friend's house with the fever. The friend's mother did not want him to leave, and at the same time, he got some bad news. The engine would not start and they ended up using an engine with 45,000 miles on it for an extra $500. He fought them on it. Eventually, Chuck and the dealer agreed on $100. Even when he is down, he is not out. Nothing holds him back from doing what is right and promoting fairness. He was all set to return to Peekskill, which if you ask me, he should have driven to his aunt's house to recoup. That would have been a 2-hour drive instead of a 7-hour drive. At least we thought. Since the mechanics rushed to fix the car they never cushioned the engine to work with the car. You must ease the engine in. He ended up driving 12 hours to get home. He started at 10 mph on back roads to Cuba, NY. From there he increased his speed to 25 mph on Rt. 17 with his blinkers on. That takes courage. Eventually, we were able to do 65 well into the trip. If I had known he was sick, I would have found a way to help him. God dang it, he is determined."

"Thank you, Mr. McNab."

"Mr. Davis, would you like to ask any questions?"

"Could another word for determined be stubborn or pig head?"

"Yeah, you could use those words. He can be stubborn like his father or me."

"Wouldn't it have taken courage and been safer to drive to his Aunt's house since he had some bad experiences on I-90?"

"It probably would have been safer seeing how he was sick. I don't know if it is courage though since he has come to my house in between the 18 wheeler and the engine kicking the bucket. In fact, the new window he had installed after the accident had the sticker "no fear" and I know he took that to heart."

"Your honor, we are done with courage, the witness may be excused" Mr. Davis comments.

If that is all, we can move on to Honesty.

Your honor, may I bring up one more Courage example about my client?

You may, but you have 2 minutes flat.

I think we should all recall why Mr. McNab is here. He protected his school from a shooter. He took the bullet, he defended the school, he risked his own life for the sake of his community. He died with courage.

Mr. Davis, would you like to counter?

Your honors, I have no words that would give a counter-argument to any justice for this last example. If there are no objects, I would like to begin the honesty portion of our trial.

You may, stated Judge Taft

Honesty

M r. Davis began, "Let's start with an obvious one in his life that the whole family now knows all about. Back when he was 10 and his brother was 6, the family took a vacation to Ontario, Canada."

I started to think to myself "Oh....I know where Mr. Davis is going....oh sugar this won't be good."

In the station wagon, both boys were arguing with each other over something quite meaningless. However, the bickering ends for a few minutes when the client's mother offered them peanuts. Most parents would think that would restore peace for a moment and it actually did. But it was the calm before the storm. After a while, the defendant asked his unsuspecting little brother if he wanted to witness a magic trick. He is 6, so of course, he would want to. He was instructed to close his eyes and your client said, "Abra Kazaam, make the peanut disappear. Then, the peanut is gone". His brother opened his eyes with pain and not pleasure. He is tried to breathe out through his nose, but the left nostril is blocked with the peanut. His brother cried for help, which prompted their parents to pull the car over on a dirt road. His mother tried black pepper and other ways to get it out, but with no luck. Unfortunately, the family did not have a cell phone, so they had to go to a local gas station to find the nearest hospital. On the way, the parents asked how it all happened and each child blamed the other. In this courtroom, we know the truth though. They get to the emergency room, Charles's mother goes in with his brother. His dad asked again how it all happened and he still maintained his story that his brother stuck it up there himself.

Charles's mother recounted how the doctor said to the nurse, "These Americans are nuts." Although that was just to have fun with a pun about the situation. His brother was punished for it and later that night when the family was at the hotel, Charles's mother cried in the bathroom thinking she could have lost a child today. All of this was because Charles played a pathetic trick on his brother.

Let's move on to when Charles was still 10. He and his brother would walk home from school together and every so often they would stop at a local deli to get a snack and sometimes even baseball cards. On four separate occasions, Mr. McNab decided to play 'buy 5 get 1 free' with the baseball card packs. He was not going to stop until one day the owner counted the packs and question him. He explained that he thought he only pulled 5 out and that he was sorry. He put one back and the transaction continued. Because of this, we can add stealing to his record.

However, it was not the only time he would steal. He is a collector of sorts. If we were to examine in-house, we would notice bath and hand hotel towels from as far as Barcelona. There might be even a robe from a hotel. He did get caught once trying to take his cousin's toy gun from Christmas when Chuck was 11 years old. However, his uncle helped him realize that Santa got the gun for his cousin. Finally, in college, there was a restaurant bench that Chuck and his roommate took for their dorm room. These are not acts of an honest person. Finally, he drank while as an underage and used a fake identification card to get into bars. Honest? I think not.

"Your honors, my client and I would like a couple of minutes to debrief before we continue. Is this possible?"

Judge Taft responded that was alright.

"Ms. Jenkins, that was hard. Those are definitely things I did. I am remorseful for some of them, but quite frankly, I am not with some others. What type of defense can we muster on this?"

"Chuck, we are going to be honest. I am going to mention some of your honest traits. When you take the stand, you will have to explain what Mr. Davis spoke about. Be prepared that the judges might ask you questions. They have the right to and this might be the start of it all."

"Thank you your honors for the 2-minute recess. I have found Chuck to be an honest man in the short time I have known him. He has owned things he has done and it takes a big person to do that. The first police officer that worked at the same school as Chuck used to play pranks. Chuck and Mike would go back and forth. One day, Charles asked the custodian to take one of the toilet paper dispensers and screw it into the wall of the officer's office. He agreed since he was a practical joker. The only thing was that the joke was on Chuck. The next day, he was double-crossed and the officer came to Mr. McNab's office and explained that a toilet paper dispenser was screwed into his desk and while doing so, it destroyed evidence in a camera for a case. Chuck's face turned white with the news. The officer boldly stated he would check the cameras to figure out who did it and arrest the person. At that point, Chuck came clean and even told the officer that he had directed the custodian and that if anyone needed to go to jail it should be him. After a few hours, they finally told him it was a joke, but he was prepared to take the fall and lose it all to protect someone else for his idea. This is one example of the many that Chuck was honest. You need to be able to add all the small success stories together. You need to know he teaches his girls and students to be honest. If you take all those factors together, I think it shows Chuck is a better person than those few acts that Mr. Davis mentioned.

As she was talking, I began to think "is that all she is mentioning?" There had to be other examples for this attribute. I need to rack my head on how I am going to get through this one. If OJ Simpson can get out of it, I should be able as well. As she was concluding, I started to get antsy in my seat. Then suddenly, it was my turn.

"Your honors. Mr. Davis and Ms. Jenkins are right about a lot of things. I stuck up the peanut in my brother's nose. I waited till college to tell my parents the truth. I was afraid that my parents would kick me out of the house or disown me. I have been ashamed of my actions for a long time. I actually used the story to teach my daughter a lesson when she stuck a Skittle in her nose. Andrew, even helped me talk to her about his experience. Yes, the baseball cards and the towels are true. I used the towels and wash clothes primarily for wrapping fragile things up. Part of my rationale was that we were paying a lot for the hotel rooms. It was wrong. There is no excuse for the baseball cards. Drinking underage, well that is a state law and I broke the law. I understand. I was also trying to fit in with my pals and have a good time. There is one critique of Mr. Davis's argument that is false. The restaurant bench was being thrown away. As it was our favorite restaurant, we recycled it to use as a seat in our room as well as storage under the bench. When I make a mistake, I own it and I reflect."

"Do you Mr. McNab? Can you give us a situation where you were wrong and owned it?" asked Judge Taft

"Judge Taft, I think there have been several times that I have owned up to making mistakes."

"In high school, a few of us were waiting for the bus. I always kept my wallet in my backpack; I just did not like how I feel having it in my back pants, especially when I am sitting. Anyway, I needed to get something out of the wallet and I noticed it was missing. There was a nice kid who liked to play a joke every so often right next to my bag. I accused him of stealing it and got into a verbal tiff. I pulled him by the shirt and broke his cross. We both got in a punch before a teacher separated the fight. I later found out that it was taken by another student who was playing a joke. I owned my mistake."

Judge Taft then said to the other two that he has heard enough. They both agreed.

Judge Wapner then told us that the court is in recess until tomorrow at 9 am.

"Ms. Jenkins, why did they stop me from talking?"

"They either liked what you said or felt you couldn't recover from what was said. I mean, you did admit to almost everything that Mr. Davis said. That was a bold tactic. Go eat and enjoy the rest of the night."

"Thank you and you do the same."

That night

I rolled into my room. Took my shoes off and viewed highlights of the day on Earth. It didn't seem to move as much time-wise. It must be slower down there than it is up here. I noticed my girls are being tucked in by Lisa. Then, I heard the conversation Lisa was having with Amanda. She feels alone. She doesn't know if she needs to get a priest and start setting up the funeral arrangements. Is that what Chuck wanted? We never spoke about it. She was then wondering how she was going to afford this place. Her parents offered for the family to move in with them since they are only a few minutes walk away. Lisa would get a lot of money for our house and that would cover her for a long time. I heard enough and was getting pretty upset. So, I decided to go get dinner.

I went to the French section of Hickey Hall and ordered one of my favorites; Chicken Cordon Blue. The waiter offered me pig's tongue to go with it and I shuttered at the thought. It brought me back to high school junior year. Thank goodness, this was not discussed as lack of courage. We were on a European trip and we stopped in Paris. At dinner, the main meal was pig's tongue. I believe everyone walked out. Some ordered Chinese food, others found a McDonalds, but Steve's father always thinks big. His cousin lived in France, sohe called her up and suddenly the three of us went out with his cousin. What a marvelous time. We ended up leaving her house at 1 am. Though I called it a house, it was a penthouse. One of my favorite moments to relive was us going to the subway. While there, we paid for our tickets, went into the tunnel and found out that the station was closed for the night. We had just missed the last train by a few minutes. We ended up walking on the Paris streets for 3 miles. We talked about everything. It was such a bonding experience. I think it made Steve and me closer friends.

As I was eating, I saw somebody walk in to eat. It was a slightly younger version of my grandfather. His sparkling blue eyes can be detected anywhere and his smile was inspiring. He built his house from scratch, a real man's man. I was so happy when I did the electric work for the building. It actually reminds me of when I had a phone reading from a psychic. Before she began, she said, "Your grandfather wants you to know that you did the electrical correctly." My hair on my arms stood up. I truly felt he has been looking over my shoulder since he passed away. He asked if we could go to the steak portion of the restaurant. It was in a cowboy-themed setting and the song that was playing at that moment was the Tennessee Waltz. It was my grandfather's favorite song. He started to sing it and he had a pretty good voice. He was so proud of me for protecting my employees and that my family was just beautiful. Grandpa was especially proud that I stayed close to my cousins because he always thought family needs to stay together. He wished that he was there to play with the girls. I thanked him for all the kind words he said on the stand and he reminded me how much he loved me. For a person who was not good at expressing emotion with words, he was doing a great job tonight. You could see the tenderness in his eyes. Grandma could not make it because just in case she gets called to the stand, they do not want her to interact with me beforehand. He said his pass to purgatory was going to expire in 20 minutes, so he just wanted me to know to relax, destress, and that he was so proud of me that I should not doubt getting into heaven. It was then getting late and I needed to be fresh for the trial tomorrow. I went back to the room and had a whiskey with ice as I felt the gentle wind on the deck. Tonight, the scenery was from Chicago when Lisa sat at a bench with a statue of a monkey. She pretended to kiss it, which a present-day Lisa would never do. It still brings a smile to my face.

Compassion

The next day, I was dressed in a Ralph Lauren slim-fit gray suit. God definitely dresses people well here. The trial was going to start with compassion. Ms. Jenkins was going to start it off. We need a big win since honesty yesterday wasn't a fight. She started by discussing how I was there for Madison throughout the whole surgery. From when they put her asleep and I was the last person she saw to holding her in my arms singing till 2 am to comfort her. She was only two, but she is my darling. This all got to the point where I have been preaching compassion over academics this year to our students. When teachers talk to me about kids failing or not attending class, I would ask have if they have reached out to the parents. Some will say they tried to reach out to the kid, some will say they reached out through email, while others will say they have called. If you have not called, then you should. You don't know if they are struggling with an illness, loss of employment, or life just sucks at the moment. Compassion is one of our values at school and this year, I would say it is the most important one. Ms. Jenkins then went on to discuss my English teacher. Tonja Bathe was probably the best 7th grade English teacher that I knew. However, she became deeply ill, but the next year was feeling better. She came back to work on a limited basis and even asked me to do an observation. During the observation, she left the room three times. The kids reacted like nothing happened because as a great teacher, she had them doing station work where she could facilitate. I met with her afterwards and all three times she went to the bathroom. It was like Willie Mays who was in a hall of fame, but the last year, you would feel pity for him every time we went up to the plate. We had a long conversation to the point where she told me some steps she put in place so she would not leave the classroom. But unfortunately, they didn't work that day. We cried and prayed. Then I had to let her know that there must be someone in the room at all times for the safety of the kids. We ended our conversation by her saying that coming to school is what heals her. I felt like I was taking that away. I rarely drank, but I know I had a stiff drink that night.

Ms. Jenkins added "After she passed away, Chuck wanted to dedicate a little free library in her honor. He kept on losing with the facilities director, but Chuck was resourceful. He found someone to donate the material. When the facilities director wanted to ensure it could not get vandalized, Chuck decided to place it outside the building where it can be filmed on two cameras. Finally, he did not lose his resilience when he got rejected again. He instead presented to the board of education which gave him overwhelming support."

Mr. Davis countered with my compassion or lack thereof to the homeless and charities. He explained that every time my wife would give donations to Good Will, I would ask for the slips to keep files. It is true, I totally did that. He went on to say that I was more concerned about my taxes than others. That is why at food drives or clothing drives, I never seemed to participate. He does not remember me ever stepping foot in a soup kitchen or helping at a library for free. It only seemed like I cared about my family and especially myself.

"If Mr. McNab could choose to buy a $300 Burberry wallet or buy clothes for a homeless center, there would be a new something, something in his back pocket. He lives life backwards. He believes he needs to have designer goods and possessions to live a happy life. He does not realize that to be happy, he needs to find himself, his identity, as well as his fellow man."

He went into the fact that when teachers asked me what grades they should give to a child, I would express to give them an honest grade. If they got a 22, give them a 22. One example was a parent's conversation I had recently before I came up here. The child missed over 20 days in the school year and we were not even in the 3rd quarter yet. He claimed it was because he had three family members pass away. hence, the reason the boy suffered with 20s and 30s for not showing up to school. I expressed that the family had my sympathies for their loss, but he exhibited these traits last year as well and probably was going to be retained if COVID did not strike. Well, Mr. Davis told the judges I should have had empathy for the family. His next claim was a mother who took both her kids to Carolina. The elementary kid transferred to another school, but the middle schooler for months was getting our services. Chuck did a welfare check. The construction crew said the kids did not live there, only a guy. When Chuck got back to the office, he called dad and told him straight up that they knew the kids moved. His son would need to enroll right away or CPS would be involved. The dad pleaded with Mr. McNab, saying how the mom was bi-bolar and hoped that the boy would come back to the father. There was no compassion here. If the son rests his head in another state, that is where the boy should go to school. His final argument is that I do not attend wakes or funerals. I did not go to my grandmothers, my aunts, or some of my beloved staff members. He is right. For all those reasons, he expressed that I am not a compassionate person.

It was my turn. I think I had this one. Well, I hope I had this one. First, I discussed Mr. Davis's claims. I admitted that if we tried everything and the student did not respond to any attempts such as extra help, not showing up, parents not communicating with us, then the child should get an accurate grade in the 2nd quarter. Does that mean that the teacher could not change later in the year if they feel the child made an improvement? The answer is no. Also, in the 1st quarter, I do believe in circle 50s, which means that any child who has lower than 50 gets a 50. As for this parent, I explained how the child had the same pattern as last year, and calling CPS on the parent would actually be a compassionate stance since they would get the necessary help. As for donations, I admitted what he said was true. I do ask for tax receipts. Why not? Why couldn't a donation also help us? If it saves a little bit of money, then we would probably buy more and cycle out the things we do not want. However, I have given food to the homeless when I was in the city. Not in a soup kitchen, but beggars who wanted money, I would give them my leftovers from a restaurant. Finally, when my secretary and her family had COVID, I brought her food, a gift card to Target and called/texted every day with her to see how she was doing. During this time, if the main office needed my sub, I let them have without complaining much and being a team player. Everyone was having a tough year, so I was compassionate to their needs.

Mr. Davis stood up and asked if could ask a question. Judge Taft allowed him to ask a question, but he had to make it brief.

"Mr. McNab, did you have compassion for Alyssa Donald when you both got back from Albany and all the cars were covered with snow. Do you remember, you just left?"

"Mr. Davis brings up a point out of context. It was my first year at a school and a teacher there asked me to attend her mother's wedding with her in Las Vegas. It was a great trip seeing the Grand Canyon, Hoover Dam, gambling, and the wedding at the little white church was unreal. I actually got to see a Vegas wedding. However, the northeast started getting snow. Soon, it was several feet of snow. Our booking ended at one hotel and we had to search for another since our flight was canceled. Can you imagine rolling your suitcase from hotel to hotel begging for a room? The internet back then did not have up-to-date prices and availability. I still remember that she was starving, but I wanted to get to the Golden Nugget, in hopes they had something. She stopped just before we got there and sat in the buffet. Like, are you serious? She was stuffy mac n cheese, meat-loaf, lettuce with blue cheese and bacon. I told her I would go to the hotel and see what they got. Surprisingly, there were two rooms left; the penthouse and a room designed for a leprechaun. I was not spending $8,000 so, I picked the other room. That night I slept in the chair since the bed was not big enough for the both of us.

The next morning, we were told we were going to Seattle. That never happened and then told we would be rerouted to Dallas, but that failed. Then we could get rerouted to Atlanta. That did not happen. Soon we had flights for Seattle and then Denver. However, all those got canceled because of the surge of the storm gripping the North East. We did not work well as a pair. She wanted to hold out and stay in Vegas while I wanted to get back. My rationale wasnot to get docked days or look bad with my new employer. The airline was able to get us to Chicago. In Chicago, they offered us flights to Philadelphia and Boston. Neither was going to work since our car was in Kennedy Airport. The airline associate told us that Kennedy, Newark, and LaGuardia would not be an option. They are all completely closed for the foreseeable future. We slept on benches and were extremely grouchy. What should have been a fun, relaxing trip started turning into a blood bath of words. While we were sleeping an attendant woke us up and told us there were two available seats to Albany. We jumped on that and ran to the boarding gate since it was going to take off in 20 minutes. On the flight, she wanted to rent a car to drive home and I wanted us to take the Amtrak. We listened to reports about the roads and it showed that the Thruway was icy. She eventually agreed to the Amtrak, but we missed it by 5 minutes. We waited for the next one which was close to three hours later. At this point, I think we stopped talking with each other. Your honors, I think it is fair to say this happens. It was a built-up stress from a unique experience. I will fast forward to when we got to her house. All our cars were completely covered with snow. We spent a long time trying to get the first couple of cars out. Luckily, a plow came by and got the first two cars out. Alyssa asked me to help her get the other two out and I said no. I needed to get home. Look, it did not end the way anyone would like. However, we both got over it and we are now Facebook friends. This was not a case of not showing compassion, but a case of two people being upset and needing space.

After my long speech to counter Mr. Davis, I politely reminded him, "When you zoom on one small act such as the Vegas crisis, you will see a struggling situation, but it is flawed representation. You need to zoom out throughout the timeline to grasp a person's compassion."

Judge Ginsberg asked Ms. Jenkins if she had any questions. She did not, but instead, she asked to call a witness; Mrs. Tonja Bathe.

"Hello, Ms. Bathe, what is your relationship with my client?"

"He was my assistant principal when I taught English. We were also on some of the same committees together."

"What are some words you would use to describe Charles?"

"He was passionate, caring, and fair."

"Can you please tell us about your observation that Charles witnessed?"

"It was a very good lesson on "A Long Walk to Water". Students did station work, were prepping for their essays, and there was some peer editing. Overall, I designed an excellent lesson."

"Would you say it was an excellent observation?"

"Not exactly. I had to leave the room three times to go use the restroom."

"After the class, Chuck and I spoke. It was a very heartfelt conversation. I will leave out some of the details as I am embarrassed by them. I hope that is alright as it has nothing to do with Chuck per se. I revealed some personal things about myself and Chuck was very supportive. Even though he was supportive, he needed to think of the well-being of my classes. He offered 504 accommodations and someone to assist me in the classroom."

"What else did he do during this meeting?"

"He knew I was scared to talk with the assistant superintendent, so he called with me to be there as a comfort."

"That phone call went very well and he was so sympathetic. This is one of the many reasons why the teachers always feel like Chuck has our back."

"Your honors, no other questions at this time."

"Mr. Davis, any questions for Ms. Bathe?"

"Your honors, no questions, but I reserve the right to call her back if needed."

"Thank you, Mr. Davis," replied Judge Wapner.

Judge Taft

As the Judges were about to motion that we would take a short recess, someone whispers into Judge Taft's ear and passes him a note. He opens the note, rolls his eyes, and asked the other two judges to meet in the chambers with him. Ms. Jenkins said this was peculiar. They asked us to wait at our tables until they came back. A few moments later, Judge Taft shared with us that he has been reassigned to another case. Even though he tried to insist to stay here, he knew we were in good hands with the other two judges. He was asked to take lead for a trial that dealt with a Congressman-elect who passed away due to COVID. The judge who was going to head the group actually had a relationship with a member of the Congressman-elect's family 60 years ago. With that being said, the other judge recused himself. Judge Wapner then suggested we break for the day and come back at 9:00 tomorrow morning.

As we were walking out, Ms. Jenkins said she never heard of a thing. She compared it to her time on Earth. She knew that if during a trial a judge got ill, they would get a sub down on Earth but never anything like this. On Earth, it would specifically go like this. If another judge was able to read the transcripts and get the general idea of the trial, then they would resume at the current point of the trial. If the case was at the end, they would go with the ruling of the previous judge. But if an appeal was needed, the new judge would seek the evidence for an appeal. However, she was just baffled by this, but she explained her focus is getting the other two judges to see that I get into heaven. If we focus on that, we would conquer. She was right that we needed to convince them, but wouldn't it be nice to have a get-out-of-jail free card? Just like when I was pursuing grants, you would lift every stone until you find something that would get you what you need. Just like what Russel had told me, people go to the library to search for miracles. Could this be my miracle?

The library was a blend of new and old. However, what was really new and old to God? I think he was appealing to all tastes when he made this. One of the first rooms I walked by was a mediation room. It had an oriental theme and felt spiritually calming. I could definitely get my Zen if I had a little time in there. Once you get past that room, you will enter the great hall. There was a giant fireplace and books that lined every other wall. There were several rolling ladders to help people get books on the higher levels. Off to the side were other rooms. Some were workrooms if people wanted a private room to study. Others had walls that you could write on to organize your ideas. Then there were other rooms with computer-like devices. The screens were on the desk wall and the keyboard was actually on the desk. The law books were in another room. That is what I would need.

In the law section, I started to tap the wood desk keyboard. I started searching ill judge, dead judge during trial, judge leave current trial, rights for accused, rights for the defendant, ways to get automatic to heaven, and even ways to avoid hell. There were some interesting results. As I scrolled through the different links of topics that supposedly connected to my request, I found odd, obscure laws. Obviously odd to me, but God must have had a reason to include it. One such law was if a judge starts to crack jokes without stopping, then the person can automatically go to heaven. It was read over 120,000 times. Just imagine how many people must have hoped, prayed, or even tried to get a judge to tell jokes during the trial. That is a Hail Mary in my eyes. Another one was that if a judge becomes ill and the case does not go in your favor, you may ask for an appeal. I didn't think anyone got ill up here though. Finally, if a judge has to leave a case while it is still in motion, a person may ask to use that as a reason to go to heaven. Bingo! I think I found it, my holy grail. I need to talk to Ms. Jenkins about this. There was no way we could talk now, so I will just wait till tomorrow. I decided to go to

Hickey Hall and have a steak and then some cheesecake. Afterwards, I went back to the hotel room, sat with an amaretto and egg nog on the deck, and looked at Lake George at sunset. My daughters were playing on the beach as the sunlight quietly left.

Next morning

The next morning, I had a conversation with Ms. Jenkins. She was very intrigued by these facts and apologized that she did not know about them.

I asked her the last time this ever happened and she said it was before her arrival, but that we needed to talk with the judges about this. This can be a fast pass to heaven. I wondered if they would just send me up given the facts I had at hand. If they don't, that means there are probably reservations about heaven.

"It is a gamble, Chuck."

"Yeah, but it is a positive gamble."

The trial resumes and immediately before we could get to treat other sections, Ms. Jenkins makes a motion to expedite heaven. Judge Wapner calls both sides up to the front.

"Ms. Jenkins, what do you mean by your motion? That is pretty ballsy."

"Your honors, under section 43 of the Binary Law, if a judge must leave for any reason, heaven is pretty much automatic."

"Your honors, I have not heard of such a thing. That means if a person kills someone and their judge leaves the trial, then the person automatically goes to heaven….that would create a bad practice."

"Alright, I heard enough. The court is in recess. I want to talk with Mr. McNab and Ms. Jenkins privately. My office now. Ruth, I will talk with you after my conversation."

Wapner's office was lined with Oakwood paneling, reminding me of those fancy parlor rooms where men in the 1930s would have a small cigar while reading their newspapers or playing pool. There was a chandler hanging in the center of the room and a beautiful antique desk where Judge Wapner did his work. One wall was filled with books stacked to the ceiling and a roaring fire was in a majestic fireplace. As we walked in, Judge Wapner was sitting on a chair in the corner of the room, reading the law.

"This is a very interesting curveball to this case."

"Well, it seems we have had a lot of interesting updates to the case, your honor," said Ms. Jenkins.

As for me, I am just trying to stay quiet.

"Your honor, I need to be able to advocate for my client in any way possible."

"Even if he wins on a technicality."

"Sir, my goal is to help my client. It is not his fault that Judge Taft left. Who knows how he would have voted? It could actually do damage to our case by not having him here. This law basically makes it a level playing field."

"Interesting way to put it, Ms. Jenkins."

As we were discussing the issue with Judge Wapner, Judge Ginsberg came in. She asked only one question, "Do you want to go to heaven."

I answered, "I would rather be with my family, but heaven is the best option I have and I will get to see my family that is up here. So yes, your honor, I want to go to heaven."

"Alright, please let both of us talk about it. You may go back to the chamber."

After 20 minutes, the trial resumed.

Treat Others

M s. Jenkins asked if she may start the next round that discussed how to treat others. We thought we had this in the bag. I was always courteous, if I did not like you I just stayed away and in general, I was a pretty polite person who was an active listener and gave advice to help people grow. I once gave a secretary who was on everyone's blacklist a major bye when she lost the money to a club in our school. Suddenly, over $1,000 disappeared. The district office wanted to find something to fire her, but I know mistakes happen. After the back and forth between the club adviser and her, I went to my boss and said the money was misplaced. He was upset because it should have been in the safe. We calmed the district office down by saying we do not know who lost it and left it at that. Three months later, she suddenly found it. It could have been her job, but I treated her with respect since she has never lost anything before. Ms. Jenkins moved on to me helping a girl with a heart issue at my school. I found grants and donations to fund 9 AEDS in the building. By law, we are supposed to have 1 no matter the size of the building. She shifted to Anderson School of Autism where I educated 18-year-old boys who were on a first-grade level. I treated them with compassion and helped them meet their goals. It was probably one of my happiest moments when one of the boys went to the mall so he could buy something and then count the change. Ms. Jenkins ended her speech by saying they are countless things she can add, but she thought everything she said speaks volumes. However, she asked to call up a witness.

Judge Ginsburg motion that she could and Willy was suddenly there.

After being sworn in, Ms. Jenkins asked him for the record of who he was and how he knew me.

"Hello, I am Willy.

"Last name please?"

"Oh, I am sorry, Willy Freer."

"How do you know Chuck?"

"Oh, we worked together for several years. He was an administrator and I was a custodian."

"Can you speak to Chuck's character?"

"Oh, he was a fun guy. We talked all the time, especially at lunch. He cared about me, his students, teachers, and his family." He seemed to reflect a lot about choices, hoping that the choices were the best. In the café, he was firm, fair, and sociable with his kids. He knew individual's struggles, knew what motivated each child, and was very respectful to his staff."

"Can you give me a time he was great with the kids?"

"He had a lot of fun time with the kids, but we had a student who just moved here from Africa. He came over here because he needed an operation and his father left both the daughter and the mother in Africa while the boy came with him to a new country. I have no idea how they picked this small town. Well, the student had a hearing device and one day, some boys were picking on him, took the hearing device, and threw it in the garbage."

"Mr. McNab witnessed this and took care of it?"

"Well, not exactly. He was in a meeting, but the boy went up to him. So Mr. McNab left the meeting to come help." By this time, the lunch period was over and the custodians were doing a deep clean of the cafeteria. He asked which garbage can, but I had already thrown everything in the dumpster."

"What happened next?"

"Chuck went in the dumpster. Shirt, tie, and all. Wait, he might have taken the tie off…I don't remember."

"And?"

"Oh, he went through bag after bag until he could find the device. I think he was taco day. You wouldn't think such a small item would be worth a lot of money, but he saved a family a few hundred dollars to buy a new one."

"Would you say he made the boy happy?"

Mr. Davis objected and said, "Your honors, she is leading the witness"

"Overruled," exclaimed Judge Wapner

Willy went on, "All I know is that the boy, the dad, the perps were all happy."

"Why the perps?"

"Mr. McNab told them they would have to pay besides being suspended."

"Thank you. Willy, that is all the questions I have for you."

Mr. Davis stood up and wanted to continue with this event.

"Good day, Willy."

"Howdy, Mr. Davis, fire away."

"First, are you situated in heaven?"

"Umm, no, I am not. I am in purgatory"

"Why is that?"

"Well, I would rather not say, the last part of my life was not great."

"Alright...well, how long are you here for?"

"Well, if I work hard and lead a good life here, I can go to heaven in 30 years. I took that plea instead of going to hell."

"30 years is a long time. It must have been something pretty bad. I know that I only ...."

"Objection, your honors, what does this have to do with our trial?"

"Sustained..."

"Alright, did you get reduced years if you testify today?"

"Actually, no, could I have? That would have been great."

The judges looked at Willy and said at this time that he couldn't."

"Let's move on...what did Chuck do with the student who threw the FM earpiece away?"

"I believe he suspended him from school and kicked him off the DC field trip."

"Did he speak with him first?"

"Yeah"

"I heard it was more like yelling."

"Now, Chuck has a lot of approaches with kids depending on the situation and the child. He was definitely pretty stern with him. However, he then gives counseling to the kid. He offered him approaches to the situation if he was not happy with Robert because of what was said in Math class. He even looked at his grades and attendance and coached him on how to make school more successful. Chuck believes every child can be successful, you just need to tap the right buttons."

"Hasn't Mr. McNab yelled at students?"

"Yes, always with reason. Such as a fight that needs to stop."

"Let's switch gears. Did Mr. McNab try to sell your car?"

"Oh, you mean my '67 Pontiac GTO.....yes, he did."

"With your permission?"

"No"

"For a price you were willing to sell it for?"

"No"

"Again, how is he a nice person who treats people well if he tried to sell your car illegally?"

"How can we say he treats people well if he tried to sell your car illegally?"

"Well, it is like this....it was a prank."

"You are OK with this?"

"I thought it was pretty funny...annoying, but funny."

"I don't understand, he didn't treat you well."

"Objection! Was not a question, but a statement" said Ms. Jenkins.

"I'll rephrase...did he treat you well in this scenario?"

"It is what it is....I pulled a massive prank on him and he was clever to list my car in the Pennysaver. I had dozens of people who wanted to buy my car. I refused them all and got a great laugh at it. If anything, it showed Chuck is smart and has a good sense of humor.

"Never mind, I have no more use for this witness."

"Well, that's a little insulting….but nice to meet you."

Judge Wapner then excused Willy.

"My side rest, your honor."

Mr. Davis was pretty ticked but stood up with a grin. That is not good I was thinking to myself.

"Well, let me first say that Chuck did show compassion for that secretary for not getting her fired for missing the $1,000. However, he went straight to the top of the district office when she let a boy suspected of selling drugs talk with his mother before being questioned. Same person, which one probably had the biggest effect on her? Couldn't he have just counseled her about what to do during an investigation? Seemed he was trying to make a statement. However, let's move on to when he was young. His grandmother drove Chuck to his Uncle Normie's dairy farm. Chuck was playing his Gameboy, Sonic the Hedgehog, I believe. His grandmother asked if Chuck wanted to be polite and go inside to say hi but he said no. A month later, Normie died.

"How about his co-worker who he has publicly said he has disdain for? She was sick with bronchitis and yet he felt she was faking it."

Mr. Davis was right. I did think she was faking it, but she is out all the time and she never uses her sick time. It was also remarkable at the same time that I was supposed to be acting principal in an elementary school and I was pulled from that because she was out. She only does what is in her best interest. She is a pusher, not a doer. My friend Lauren would say to me that I can't complain if I am going to do the work. Well…I always went back to what was the best interest of the child. For example, the guidance counselor came to me about a parent meeting for one of my colleague's students because she wanted someone who would actually care about the whole situation and have ideas instead of repeated others' ideas. We once read a book called "Shifting the Monkey" and she took that book to heart but to the 100th degree. I wonder if she would be different if I ever mentored her like I mentored others. The problem was that she said in her interview that she was only giving us two years, which was a stepping stone to a superintendency. So, she had her plan already in motion. I don't know why I am letting this get to me. I wish Lisa was here in my corner. She would calm me down, take deep breaths and let me see the reality. She would tell me to keep my head up high even when the worst is before my very feet. It feels like my worst nightmare that someone would use Sally as an argument to keep me from heaven. I just need to remember to take my breaths, keep a smile on my face, and be ready to present why I should go to heaven. If Lisa wasn't a 10 out of 10, she certainly was a 9.99.

"How polite was Chuck? In junior year, Chuck had a steady relationship. In fact, the dorm called them prince and princess of Doyle as they were magical together. She was the first and only girl that Chuck's parents would meet until Lisa became the love of his life. Why am I telling you this? In college, Chuck's girlfriend cheated on him. Yes, that is awful and obviously, she meant a lot to him. She lost her virginity at a party that Chuck was not at."

Shit, he went here. This was probably the lonely point in my life. After she did what she did, I thought I was worth nothing.

"The case could be made that she and her friends went over to socialize and she was not a real drinker. Shit happens and Kat drank too much and let a guy coax her to acts that would ruin her relationship with Chuck. She tried to make amends but he would have nothing to do with her again. He avoided her at the dining hall, in the dorms, everywhere they intersected at college. Soon, she realized she was not going to convince Chuck to come back. Chuck was not happy when she tried to makeup and he was not happy when she moved on. He became a prick to his friends. Then he was having a conversation with a girl at a bar. By the way, just a point of reference, he was underage. They flirted even though she mentioned she had a boyfriend. Then, he broke up the relationship. After their first encounter, he was happy. He was happy not because of her, but because he torpedoed a relationship. This happened after he vowed to break up other people's relationships and date the girls. He was so successful that in 1 semester he broke up 13 relationships. Is that someone who treats people nicely? Karma came and he learned his lesson in Delaware when a boyfriend came searching for Mr. McNab in the Embassy Suites hotel, but the damage was already done."

"Judges, do you mind if I ask Chuck a question?"

"He is still under oath". Replied Judge Ginsberg

"Ms. Jenkins, are you alright with this?" asked Judge Wapner

With a nervous and yet calm voice, Ms. Jenkins replied, "Judge Wapner, I am sure whatever question Mr. Davis has will eventually come out. So, he may ask."

Mr. Davis then asked his question. As he was asking the question, I started to think that we have been doing the trial, but why was I getting so nervous with the suspense. Is it a light out, KO question?

"Chuck, are you with us right now? I will repeat the question. How did you break all these relationships up? What type of charm, spell, or evil device did you use?"

"Sir, I used ice cream"

"Excuse me? Did I hear you straight? If I recall some of your conquests, your prey were at bars. You went to get them ice cream at the bar? This is work of Satan himself."

"Objection" screamed Ms. Jenkins.

"Mr. Davis, Ms. Jenkins was kind enough to allow you to ask a single question that you requested, but showboating with the added lip will not get you what you desire. Do I make myself clear?" expressed Judge Wapner.

"Yes, your honor"

Judge Ginsberg looked perplexed. "Chuck, for my own sake, can you please dive deep into that two-word answer? You know that should be broken down else you will sound as if you are a witch doctor of sorts."

Glad Lisa was not here to witness this. We all have our skeletons in our closet and this was mind. Sounding defeated, Chuck stated, "Your honors, I am ashamed of this. I would ask someone what their favorite ice cream was. For example, if I asked Jane Doe and she said Mint, I would then ask her how does she know it is her favorite unless she tried others like Butter Crunch, Twist, etc. I summed it up as there was more to the story, but that is the general gist."

Mr. Davis sounded triumphant and finished his dissertation on how I treated others.

"How did Chuck treat his best friend, not just once but twice in their long history? When his friend Steve told him he was having a boy and his girlfriend had delivered their child, sure Chuck was surprised. The reason why Chuck was never told was because the girl was his ex-girlfriend. He did not talk to Steve for over 3 months after that. He would not return phone calls, emails, or text. They patched things up, but was he around for his friend when he was caught in a scandal? No, he never visited once. What type of friend does that? Or what person puts denature alcohol in someone's eye? When Chuck worked at Walmart, he liked to have fun and pull pranks. He was about to spray a friend's back, but the gentleman turned around and struck in the eye. Immediately, he was rushed to the hospital. Surprisingly, Chuck did not lose his job, but that is not a way to treat anyone. Chuck claims to be a good friend and treats everyone really well. If that is the case, then why did he treat a very close friend pretty awful after the blowout with Dino? His secretary was a confidant. However, after she left his office, he avoided her. He would see her in the hall and he would duck into a classroom. He would let her calls go to voicemail. She would come to the office and he would say he was busy. Is that how to treat others?"

"Chuck, it is your turn."

"Your honors, Mr. Davis brought up a lot of examples that I would like to clarify. Steve is still my best friend. In fact, he just asked me to be the Godfather to his unborn child. We are friends, we are best friends, and in fact, we are brothers. Families fight and unfortunately, when he told me about the first child, I was excited for him. Then to see he had it with my ex broke the bro code. I still supported him, but when I get upset, I do isolate myself. It is the way I handle myself when big negative things happen. When he was involved in the last scandal, I called and texted him to make sure he was alright. He did not want to make it a big deal. However, I knew how to be a friend to him because I know him too well. As for my uncle, I regret not saying hello to him. I was 13 maybe, I do not recall, but I think about it frequently. It is part of the reason I encourage my kids to always talk to family. I took my mistake and made it a learning experience for my kids. As far as college, I was in a very dark place. I have no excuse. It was wrong and one of the ex-boyfriends definitely put me in my place. As far as the secretary, I was given strict orders to let the district office assistant superintendent know the minute she made a minor mistake. I glossed over a lot of her mistakes, but this child was going to go to a superintendent's hearing until the mom told the boy to stay quiet until she got there. There was a lot of "yes mom" from the boy while the mom did most of the talking. Yes, I was angry. We have been searching for the dealer for a while and we finally caught him and he wouldn't talk. Eventually, we let him go and the drugs kept on being sold. I have also wondered if the mom knew her medication always disappeared or looked empty."

"Lastly, something I regret is about Janet, my last secretary. She was more than a secretary. She was my right hand and could finish my sentences. She is one of the very few people that could prank me and have taught me a lesson at the same time. Honestly, now she calls anyone else but me when she needs help. She would call my new clerical for my passwords, so she doesn't need to speak with me. It is amazing how one situation in September ruined a complete friendship."

Judge Wapner then asked, "Please explain yourself about the prank and teaching a lesson, that seems peculiar."

"Yes, your honor. I want to be a perfectionist when I send out emails or public letters. I was writing a letter to the parents throughout the district and had her proofread it. She told me I could send it and then after a minute, she told me there were a couple of spelling mistakes that needed to be edited. My jaw dropped. I scrambled to find a way to get the letter back, but it was already sent. Then she started to laugh. I asked her what was so funny and she first said I was pranked, but then explained that you can't be such a perfectionist. When you do that, you get paralyzed with guilt and trauma for spelling a word wrong. You need to show more self-compassion to yourself."

Judge Wapner then interrupted again by saying "You know Mr. McNab, that was a very good point she had. Alright, please continue with your original thought about Janet and your regrets."

"The situation was handled badly your honors. Prior to the bad situation, she told me that she would not forget my birthday. She would make sure one person would remember my birthday. Then on my birthday, she did not do a thing. No text, call, email, or a stop by to say hello. I was not upset she forgot about the birthday; I was upset because I thought she didn't want to be a friend. So then yes, I avoided her because I did not want to have awkward interactions. So, I thought having no interactions was better than awkwardness. I was becoming numb to the situation. When my mom had open-heart surgery, I realized how much I missed her. I could have lost her and my mom. I have to work to let go and accept while realizing that everything in life adapts. We were trying to work things out until this happened.

Mr. Davis stood up and asked if he could ask a question.

"Proceed," asserted Judge Wapner.

"Mr. McNab, how else did you act when you lost your precious secretary?"

"Umm....to deal with my shame of being by myself, I withdrew from the public eye. I stayed in my office, silencing my opinions so that my boss would not take anything more away from me. I got the message to Janet that she was not to come over to my office because Dino wanted her solely in her new office. That was true, but I also couldn't take seeing one of my best friends. I now realize this prevented me from being my true self."

"Thank you Mr. McNab for explaining again that you do not know how to treat people properly."

"Mr. Davis, that is twisting my words. Was I wrong? The answer is yes, but I retreated into myself. I did not want the public to see how I was and I focused solely on my work. I needed to work on my self-compassion, but at that time I lost my secretary, a new job opportunity, and was sucker-punched with more job responsibilities because I was great at my job and my one colleague can't hold her weight. If you look at the whole picture, I treat my students like they are my own. I give parents advice on how to make their kids successful. I am always polite to people I interact with. In fact, as I was leaving for school and almost at my car, a parent stopped by to get something from the building. I went back to help her. I truly care for people. Lastly, I wanted my students to walk into a cheerful place, and my kids to their sidewalk chalk to make signs welcoming my students."

Character

⟡

M r. Davis started this round by discussing my stress level. Yes, I bear a lot of stress. He said that when I was stressed, I ate peanut butter cups like they are never going to sell them again. He went so far as to mention how I ate 5 bags in 3 days at work because I was so upset about losing my secretary. I craved them so much, I had a whole collection of apparel of Reeses's from my boxers to my sweatshirt. He claimed it was disgraceful to worship a piece of food. Besides being stressed, he said I was stubborn. When I lost my secretary, I told them not to give me another one. I will work all by myself and become a hermit. When I know something is not fair, I can be stubborn as well. Probably being stubborn is not a good character trait. Mr. Davis went on to say I did not always take in the moments of life and I really should have since there were a lot of pleasant things in my life I took for granted. For example, times when my daughter wants to sit on my lap and I just want to do schoolwork. Take time for the little things. He mentioned how I also always wanted the next step and not soak up the joy of the little moments. He said if I did, it could change the outlook of my overall life including work, family, and especially success. Was the guy who is trying to put me in hell saying I was successful? He was right that I always wanted to advance. I am an AP, I want to be principal, and then superintendent one day. He told the judge that I failed to take pleasure in my current job. The funny thing though is that he also twisted my dedication to being an AP. He claimed because I felt so comfortable in my school community and my job, I self-sabotaged opportunities for growth which in turn caused my stress and lack of character.

Ms. Jenkins then went. First, she started discussing the time the administration danced to the YMCA even though I am not a dancer in any shape or form. I did it because it pleased the audience. I helped set up PBIS to help transform the school into a positive culture. I was not a yes man like a few people in my district, but an honest person who would say yes if that was the right answer and no if there was nothing that could be done. I can see both sides of an argument and try to be fair in the decisions that I make. For example, when there was a fight this year between two special education boys, I heard both sides and then coached them through the issues at hand. I do confess to God and I pray as well.

She continued, "Finally, he tries to lead by example. He practices gratitude. He will go up to a person and explain why he is grateful for them. For example, the day that sent Mr. McNab up here, he offered gratitude to the bus drivers for driving in the cold weather and ensuring that our children stay safe. When his doctor told him to ban the candy, his new secretary hid it all so he could not find it. He has gone over a month with only 2 sneaks of chocolate. He gave specific gratitude for her actions."

However, after her dialogue, she called my Aunt Kathy to the stand.

"Hello, can you introduce yourself?"

"Yes, I am Kathy Veer, Chuck's aunt."

"How was your relationship with him?"

"We had a nice, beautiful relationship. We loved to talk genuinely and about funny things. We would stand next to the washing machine in my kitchen and chat away about family, love, current events, and dreams."

"Would you say he was a serious person?"

"He was always very ambitious and never wanted to do anything wrong. We came to his hotel when he was visiting England on his high school trip. We took him out and at a traffic light, I asked him if he wanted to take a picture. He was good with that, and as we were taking the picture I tried to get him to drink beer. You can tell he was not pleased. He did not want to break any laws."

"Anything else you would like to add?"

"He loved to read. Whenever he came over, he had another Harry Potter book he would finish. He was always polite to our friends and if he saw someone by himself, he would go over and talk whatever they wanted to talk about."

"When I was ill, he would call and check up on me. Back then international calls were still expensive, but he would do it. Family forever."

"Thank you for your time."

"Mr. Davis, do you wish to ask Kathy Veer any questions?" asked Judge Ginsburg

"Only a couple, your honors."

"Did he come to your funeral?"

"No."

"That doesn't sound like he cared about you?"

"The family decided that one person would pay the outrageous price the airline was demanding. American Airline was charging over $2000 round trip. I knew he wanted to be there, I know the whole family wanted to be there. I looked at the channels from purgatory at that time. He was crying over my death and praying to God that I go to heaven."

"When Mr.McNab did come to visit you, how did he look?"

"He always looked tired. I would tell people it was the plane ride, but I knew it was more."

"What do you mean?"

"For a youngster, he didn't know how to relax. He was always anxious to get his goals done. He placed high expectations on himself, but it was unhealthy."

"That is definitely a character flaw. No other.."

"Pardon me...that is not a character flaw. He set targets for himself, as he had the diligence and determination to conquer the objectives and he believed in himself. When faced with a problem, he would think outside the box to find an alternative way to succeed. He put in the hard work, I just wished he relaxed more than he did."

"No other questions, your honor. Wait, I am sorry, I do have one more question. Do you think Chuck ever lived in the moment?

I mean, you say he was always focused, but did he enjoy or soak up the events of his life?"

"Mr. Davis, that is a very hard question to answer. I saw him laugh, cry, and smile. I know he didn't lead a sheltered life in that he explored too much. If there was something he wanted to do, he did it."

"Mrs. Veer, that did not really answer my question, but maybe you are right, that is a question for Mr. McNab."

"Mrs. Veer, you are free to go about your business. Thank you for your time."

It was my turn. I felt that Ms. Jenkins had summed it up nicely. Mr. Davis explained that I did not live in the moment all the time. He was right, but I remember the smiling face of Madison as we are taking long walks playing the letter game with princess names. For example, A is for Ariel and when I mess up with the letter "d" she starts laughing and says "oh daddy." I remember when sitting on the couch with Nicole and she talks about history as though she is an expert. This made me so proud of her or when she builds a tray. Those are the little memories that are huge. Suddenly, all the fighting that goes on disappears because I have my two little princesses there. So, Mr. Davis is right to an extent, however, I have cherished a lot of little moments in the past. If you take a look at me now, I am a different person in each of my chapters. You soak up the moments I think differently. The younger version of myself reflected flying a plane, holding the wheel over a bountiful amount of green trees, and thinking I am controlling a bunch of metal flying. Sitting on the brown recliner as Whiskey, my American Esmiko, sat on my lap as the ball dropped. It is a moment I will never forget. One of the greatest bonds a person can have is with his dog. When I became a father, I never took for granted all the times that I thought would always be here with my kids. I might have rushed through bike rides, walks, or eating dinner, which is actually true. Do I remember the times where Nicole and I made a game of throwing the dirty laundry into the baskets on the first floor? Absolutely. Do I recollect how she met Aaron Judge and she kept running towards him to get a high five. I will always remember that. I will always recall my girls' faces when they met all the Sesame characters, when Lisa got to dance on stage with Cookie Monster, and when Madison got to talk with Arial at Disney World. All these moments are burned into my mind, and realizing they are gone, do I wish I might have slowed down even more? The answer is yes, but my understanding that I should have slowed down is different than not appreciating the times you have with loved ones.

I know I am supposed to support my reasons for going to Heaven, but I wouldn't be true to everyone here if I did not add that I wished Lisa and I did more than speed dating after we had Nicole and Madison. We rarely went out on dates, but when we did we rushed through dinner so we could get back home. We had this to perfection as we already knew what we wanted when the waiter came to say hello. Apps and desert rarely happened. After dinner, we could never decide what to do next. It was almost like we lost how to communicate without the girls around. We were always ready for the phone to ring, a text of some sort, or a problem we had to figure out, like our refinancing company messing everything up. I couldn't recall at times how our community or even Route 9 looked with lights on. It was rare for us to be out at 5 pm. The dates I remember always consisted of Lisa's infectious laugh and holding hands. That laugh reminded me of when we first started dating. On our second date, I did say to her that she would only have me at a max of 5 months since I don't date anyone more than that. She looked directly into my eyes and said I will be marrying you. At that moment, I did not feel like the self-imposed rental that I had become. I felt love and belonging, I felt like I was worthy of love.

There is no denying that I am looking to be promoted. Honestly, I can compare it to the malls. When I was little, the JV Mall looked huge. As I grew up, it started to become small, like a person outgrows their shoes. I moved on to a bigger mall the Poughkeepsie Galleria because it had more options and expanded my mind. Then you outgrow that to the point that Woodbury Commons is the next size up. I outgrew being a teacher and now as an AP, I have outgrown this because I am ready for more. I am ready to help more students and parents out. I have been ready; I just haven't found the right fit yet. However, a joyful life at work isn't made up of a couple of decisive events. It is a string of daily experiences that encompass trust for your colleagues, open canvas conversations, and gratitude for the little and big moments. The little moments are like getting Jose in a public school close to his house while a big moment is watching your kids that you oversaw for four years graduate. A joyful life has inspirations such as Richy getting his diploma when all the odds were against him due to his health and having faith. There are plenty of times that faith was what was needed. For example, faith that the 9th grader who was pregnant would still find a way to get her education. As for being stubborn, I can be, but I feel like most times I am not. When you believe in something so strongly, you should be stubborn. I also think I offer a lot of flexibility. People can sway me to different viewpoints if they present evidence. I think Mr. Davis's claim is absurd that it makes me a bad person or a person not worthy of heaven. God created us with flaws. A strong person tries to overcome the flaws to make his life, his families' lives, and the world a better place. I think I have done that. Thank you for giving me time to speak.

Insecurity

M r. Davis then spoke. "Your honors, we have discussed the areas that normally determine if a person goes to heaven or hell. However, for the subject in question, I would be remiss if I did not bring up another area that goes to his core. That is his insecurity."

"Your honors, I object. We were given no notice of this. If they wanted to talk about it, why did they not bring it up in character where it would fit?"

"Our view is that it is a very important manner that deserves its own proper discussion. In section 34 of the statute, if deemed necessary as a core theme, either side may request to have the theme highlighted as its own section of the trial. Your honors, what do you say?"

Judge Wapner addressed the courtroom and told Mr. Davis he could proceed, but also reprimanded him for not giving notice to Ms. Jenkins to prepare a proper defense.

"Ms. Jenkins, do you want to adjourn to solidify your argument on this portion of the case?"

"Chuck, what do you think?"

"I don't know how we would prepare. Insecurity is my biggest issue."

"Any witnesses we should call?"

"Can we let him proceed and call someone tomorrow if needed?"

"Your honors, we will allow Mr. Davis to proceed today. However, we would like to have a rebuttal witness called tomorrow if needed."

"Ms. Jenkins that will be fine" stated Judge Ginsburg.

"Judge Wapner, I call up the defendant."

"Chuck, go up there and be yourself. Don't analyze what he is asking, answer from your heart. You have been up there a lot, so you know how it works."

"Mr. McNab, do you believe you fit in with people or that you belong with people?"

"I never thought about that. I have friends that range in different personalities. I would not be honest to myself that I am shy. I tried to find friends. For example, I met my college roommate at orientation, and partly because I was afraid I would not find someone else, I asked him to be my roommate for the fall term. I definitely did things to fit in with other people and would curb my personality so that they accepted me."

"Mr. McNab, you do realize that it is healthier to be in the belonging category. People accept you for who you are. It requires us to be who we are. It seems you went for acceptance and that was a very good example you gave, but it also proves the insecurity that you possess.

"Sir, please tell us about your friendships," demanded Mr. Davis.

"I have a lot of friends…a few very close ones, but a lot of people I consider to be friends."

"Sir, let's clarify….do you consider them friends or friendly? Are they your friends because you fit in with them or because you belong?"

"Ummm….I don't know. I have a lot of people who I can chat with."

"So is that friends or friendly? You haven't answered the question, sir?"

"I don't know Mr. Davis. I think I have friends and a lot of people with whom I am friendly with. I think most people have very few close friends and those were definitely because they accepted me because of who I am. I used to go to the Poconos with a few buddies, those were close friends. I wouldn't have dreamed to invite most people I know to stay in a cabin with me eating just hot dogs, hamburgers, chicken, ribs, etc. the whole time. You do something like that with your best friends."

"Do you doubt your friendships?"

"Yes, yes I do."

"Have your friends told you not to doubt?"

"Yeah, but I love to analyze. I watch, I listen, and I am very good at seeing details."

"Maybe a little too good…."

"I think it is fair to say through watching video on you and your listening to your thought process, you daily doubt certain friendships. Such as why you did not get a Christmas card from a person to why someone skipped your hallway while walking through the whole building?"

"Counsel, is that a question?"

"Sorry, I'll take that back.

"No, I will answer. I would feel so much better talking out my feelings, trusting people who say they are there with me. They do not necessarily have to talk, but their actions let me know I am not alone. There are very few people I trust at that level. When I do and then I see red flags, it makes me doubt."

"Is it true that you are friends with Tom and Lauren at work?"

"I would say so."

"Do they accept you for who you are or because you fit it?"

"I think we gel. I still question the lines of the friendships. However, I think they have seen my imperfect self. I have been authentic in front of them and heck, I would hope the same is true for both of them. I will say that I do joke with them when I feel awkward by being authentic and showing my vulnerability. However, Tom really showed his true colors when I felt like I was defeated earlier this year. I started to numb my negative emotions by constantly doing work and eating chocolate. When you start to numb your negative emotions, you also numb the positive ones as well."

I stopped myself because listening to how I shut myself down really upset me. Hearing the words made it all come back to life. I was self-protecting, but now looking at the whole experience, to grow, I must be honest with myself and also forgiving. After some deep breaths, my tears vanished, and I continued.

"I was not interacting with my sarcastic math teacher, wouldn't talk hot sauces with one of my ELA teachers, and stopped talking sports with a guidance counselor. Everything I did was based around work. Tom would not let the door close on him, he earned his spot to listen to my vulnerabilities and imperfections because I know once the door opens, he would be a vault. There are people that are only there for the good times, then you have friends who help guide you through the dark tunnels. He helped me see the positive. Finally, would Tom really fart in front of me if he wasn't being authentic?"

"Mr. McNab, he could have just been an ass. Let's move on about your work?"

I paused for a second and after hearing that dialogue, I realized something. I should not have to be guarded with them. They wouldn't be my friends unless they wanted to be. These attack questions have actually made me less anxious about my friendships. We look after each other like the three musketeers.

"What about my work, I know I have done a great job with everything I do."

"Do you need people to proofread your work?"

"Majority of the time I have my secretary proofread my work because I do not like to proofread."

"Do you need to be assured when it comes to your work?"

I think there was a point that I needed to. When I was given a fourth year towards tenure, that threw me out of whack. I always did my job, but you grow from experiences and I think that sequence of events made me a stronger person. By the way, that 4th year was not because I couldn't do my job. It was because I never believed a person needed to be in the spotlight. I did not believe I needed the credit, we need what we needed to do for our kids and community. Our actions should represent who we are.

"Exactly, and yet you would seek advice from people before you did something. You never seemed to trust your strong internal instinct. You always wanted a guarantee, knowing that people supported your viewpoint, yet your intuitive voice was always pretty accurate."

"Well, Mr. Davis, you are right to an extent. There are plenty of times that I listen to my gut, but when it comes to the success of my kids, I believe a team can strengthen any idea."

"What I heard your honors is that he agrees."

Well, I agree that I sought advice. There are always other perspectives that must be weighed into a decision before implementing it. For example, when I switched 20 teachers' rooms around, I sought input from the teachers' union, the teachers, and the facilities. It wasn't for reassurance, it was to get by and also do the best decision possible. It is just like JFK who surrounded himself with the most gifted and talented people to share ideas and create the best strategies. You have to know your strong and less strong characteristics.

"One last question on this topic. Do you constantly reflect on how you can either please people or make them happy?"

"Yes, Mr. Davis, I do. I cannot deny that. I love to reflect. 2020 was a rough year and so many people have dark clouds over their heads. If I can make people happy with scavenger hunts or finding the golden tickets or dressing up as a coffee cup, then I will. Yes, what you are trying to get to is that I lost a really good friend this year. He thought I was angry with him and I thought he was angry with me too. We didn't talk for a month and then we both thought each other moved on. We had a conversation and cleared the air, but it is still very awkward. A lot of things that use to happen like text messages or talking about our families didn't happen anymore. Do I reflect? Absolutely. Do I want to make things better? Yes, but I didn't know how. Is it hard for me to believe him when he says everything is better? Yes, because it isn't the same. I must realize that things won't be the same, but we are still friends. I think most people reflect or hope they could keep a friendship that was destroyed by miscommunication."

"Let's talk about another topic. What is your ethnic background?"

"I am proudly Scottish, Goan, and Portuguese. A mutt is the finest sense."

"That's great. American has been made up of all ethnic backgrounds. We should all be so proud to learn the traditions, customs, and languages of our families. Would you agree?"

"Absolutely, we are a melting pot and should not forget about cultures." Why do I feel like I am about to get trapped in something?

"So, do you own a bagpipe or a kilt?"

"No, but I always wanted to wear a kilt when I was young for my wedding. To represent my Scottish roots would have been fantastic."

"Did you ever think of wearing a Sherwani?"

"What is that?"

"That is an Indian wedding suit usually made of silk and it is embroidered with stones on it."

"That is good to know. I am sure I have seen them before."

"This proves my point though that you do not know your mother's heritage."

"Is it true you never acknowledged your heritage when you were little?

"That is true. There were only whites and blacks at my school at the time and it was hard being the only tan kid. That is why I focused just on my Scottish roots."

Mr. Davis was right. I tried to distance myself from my true self. That part of my life just did not determine if I was going to fit in with the crowd. In that world, in my elementary school or later at the private minute Catholic school, I did a lot of pleasing and proving my worth to kids I wanted to be friends with. Funny how I don't stay connected with anyone from those times.

I continued with my answer to Mr. Davis. "I would get made fun of based on my skin tone and people would even accuse me of being adopted and that my father looks like Santa Claus. To be accepted for being me, I had to conform."

"How many languages does your mother know?"

"Well, she knew 6."

"Did she offer to teach you?"

"Yes, but I wasn't ready."

"Were you not ready or did not want to learn?"

"I wish I had learned the languages when I reflected on it as an adult."

Even now, this pains me. Every time I think of that chapter of my life, new ideas emerge. Imagine if I had accepted myself back then. My mom was never trying to make me stand out. She wanted me to be proud. I wish I could give my mom a big hug and apologize for not receiving all the gifts she tried to provide for me.

Mr. Davis concluded with "Your honors, I rest."

"Your honor, can we take a recess to talk with my client and gather witnesses if needed?"

"Yes, you may," Judge Wapner stated. "Court is in recess until tomorrow at 9 am."

Post adjournment

I went up to my hotel exhausted, not wanting to do anything else. As I was walking into the lobby, I noticed something that should have been so obvious. Between the entrance to the hotel and the second set of doors were tourist guide packets. You know, those types you see when you go to Lake George that says $2 off A&W or on the Minnie Ha Ha. Here they had packets about the different activities that are offered each day. They also have a sign-up sheet to do different events. For today, there was a sign-up sheet for a hike in the nearby mountains. It was already 1 pm and it starts at 4. I ordered room service, which literally takes about 15 minutes to get there. A beautiful steak with garlic mash potatoes and green beans. I ate on my deck overlooking Niagara Falls from the Canada side. The Sheraton over the Falls is by far the best hotel in Niagara. My family had a great July 4th there once. With the red, white, and blue colors underneath the falls at night and fireworks littering the sky. As I was reliving this moment, I got a call on my arm that Ms. Jenkins wanted to meet me. There goes the plan to go hiking, but I would say she was more important than anything else now.

Ms. Jenkins wanted my opinion on how to approach the counter-argument. My initial thought was to tell her that we should look at things I have asked opinions about. I knew something was wrong and needed the right players involved. She wanted to know if there was anyone up here who could vouch for me. Sophia could. She could discuss how we wanted to make the lobby safer and I asked her opinion about my plan. My plan was to put the staff members' entrance on the opposite side of the lobby so that parents could not just enter. Thinking about that makes me chuckle since I died because a staff member let an intruder in. Anyway, I asked her opinion on it since she lived in the lobby every day. Ms. Jenkins thought that would squash that argument of Mr. Davis, but what about my insecurity when it comes to friends? I did not have an answer for her. I have been to a therapist who gave me techniques, I knew it was a problem, but I also considered myself fat throughout my whole life when there were times I was the skinniest person around. Bad events leave scars on you that might never heal. When I was young, I was fat, threw up after running 5 feet, was always sick, and probably used a nose booger thing for the longest of times. It was hard for me to have friends and the ones that I had, I would find ways to keep. Even though I had scars, my confidence grew during college. Being a DJ allowed people to hear my voice without seeing my body. You wouldn't believe I was 150 pounds until my senior year of college. I started subbing and really well in love with teaching. For some reason, I was able to connect with older generations but had a hard time with my generation. I was not a clubber. I liked to stay local unless I was traveling to an exotic place. Also, I loved to work to save up money. I hoped her idea would work. Honestly, what else could I do?

It was now 3:30. I still had time to make the hike. The bus was going to leave at 3:45. I was about to take a quick shower, but remember you don't get dirty or smell here. I open up the closet and notice a hiking outfit. I was outside of the hotel at 3:40. Once I got on the bus, this Aussie sat next to me. We started chatting, and he was an accountant until he realized the joy he was lacking. Soon he became a dancer on the cruise lines. He was able to travel anywhere in the world while dancing with senior citizens. I asked what type of rooms he got on the ships, but he said they were nothing to write home about. You shared your room with 5 other people, 3 bunk beds up. One of his roommates on several rides always had a habit of putting on his underwear on wrong because he got dressed in the dark, so as not to wake us up at 2 am.

I asked him what it was like going from accountant to being a dancer of the seniors. He explained that he would work on major clients' accounts, but that people will soon get laid off due to the company mainstreaming things. Even though that was the case more and more work rested on his shoulders. He started to under-function. He would ask for assistance on minor things that he learned as a first-year accountant. People were perplexed that he took long lunches and breaks in the coffee lounge. People started to gossip and his bosses started talking about letting him go. Then his boss suggested he talk with someone about what is going on.

His shrink indicated that it was stress and anxiety. She asked him if he thought the work was meaningful and Aussie as I called him said it paid the bills. Then, the most remarkable question was asked of him and that was, does he play at all? He questioned her and she explained playing affects our brain, cultivates empathy, and can circumnavigate intricate social groups. It permits the body to distribute endorphins, which are the body's biological feel-good chemicals. His therapist went one step further and really dived deeply into the act of playing. Play is unique to each person as one person might like to read a book, another draws comics, while another person might like to run a marathon. If a person like me (since I love playing pranks) plays at work, it can enhance productivity and increase job satisfaction. Playing, especially with someone else building a bonding experience. However, if someone is not playing, then the opposite is happening, which is going into a depression, just like the Aussie was doing at his job. His therapist suggested that his work needs to be meaningful for him and should utilize his gifts. She asked him what he used to do for fun when he was younger and he said he always danced and loved to travel. He also mentioned that last year he did a version of dancing with the stars at his work and noticed his productivity increased dramatically and that he was even whistling at work. The next session his therapist brought a newspaper with an ad circled on it. A local cruise line needed experienced dancers to teach classes on their cruise ships. The rest was history. That was the best part of his life and he would still be doing it if he didn't choke on a piece of steak.

The hike instead was entertaining. The foliage was beautiful and the stream we hiked nears was beautiful. Animals drinking from the water and squirrels racing nuts up a tree reminded me of the

Hudson Valley. Once we got to the top of the mountain, there was a plateau. Kids were playing, and just beyond the kids was a small wooden stage with people acting. It was two people and they looked like they were having fun, not being serious at all. As I sat on one of the wooden benches, the voice of the male became very familiar to me. I couldn't tell by how he dressed who he was since he had a costume on, but I was very sure I have heard the voice before. The woman was fun to watch, doing a scene from Raisins in the Sun. Afterwards, the two thanked each other and the woman ran off to see her friends. The gentlemen took off his face mask, grabbed a bottle of water from his rucksack, and sat on a boulder. I recognized him and was gitty to meet him.

I introduced myself and at first, he was very cold. Articles I have read about him have mentioned how he was a cold, hardened person who wouldn't sign autographs for his fan base unless he made money on it. I wasn't going to ask for an autograph to add to my collections since it wouldn't do any good. I asked him what he was reflecting on at the boulder. He said he was trying to put his life in perspective. He became an actor by accident and people didn't realize he always cared about the money after he noticed how poor his family was while he was growing up. His father was a truck driver and his mom a maid. He had to drop out of school at 13 to make money for the family and since that day, he valued every penny he could get his hands on. He told me though people don't realize he valued money, he didn't want to see other children in Scotland get raised without education and donated his entire salary for two movies to create a foundation to educate Scottish children. He thought there was no more noble profession to helping kids grow. He thanked me for my service and all I could think of was that he was my favorite 007. He was going back to the bus, then he asked if I wanted to tag around afterwards for a whiskey since tomorrow was his verdict day. I obliged.

After getting back to the hotel later than I planned, I heard on knock on my door and a British voice "let me in, Chuck…bloody hell, open the door". It was my Aunt Kathy from my mom's side of the family. She heard how the last part of the trial went after her portion and wanted to assure me that things will go the way I want them to go. I just need to have faith and a whiskey. She loved her whiskey and tea. We went down to the bar to chat. I was still saddened that I did not go to her funeral. My first real experience with my aunt was when they visited us in Peekskill. I was playing a soccer game and they walked me home. My aunt told me when I got home that I must take a bath and I did not want to. My uncle chased me throughout the house while I tried to call my mom to get her to side with me. Well, that did not work out well. Nevertheless, as time went by through the years, I enjoyed spending a lot of time with my aunt. She was a sage in many ways. She pondered the universe differently than most and you could tell she hid a lot of dark ghosts in her past. I asked her what were her turning points that her movie reel showed her and she mentioned my grandfather's assassination. He was a wealthy cashew nut plantation owner in Zanzibar. During the revolution, his property was taken away and while defending it, he was murdered. With that single event, the arranged marriage that was planned for both my aunt and my mother was void. If he was never murdered, she would now be the owner of the plantation and still be in Zanzibar. Yet, she would never have changed that portion of her life. She had three beautiful children out of it. I apologized to my aunt for never wanting to know about my Goan and Portuguese roots when I was young. I was too ashamed. I explained that I had to disregard my heritage so I would not be scorned by the white and African American kids.

"There, there dear. It is alright. Children try so hard to fit in, especially when they are blind to their core. But once you realize this and correct your path, all will be alright. Chuck, my love, whatever happens, remember to breathe and laugh."

I thought to myself that laughing in hell is no funny matter, but I asked her to clarify. Sometimes I needed multiple attempts at their British logic.

"Remember your breathing exercises my boy. You did your best when you had some silence in your life and you just took a breath. I know it can be hard and a bloody pain in the ass. You want to do, you like your do list, but take in the silence. With the silence, also remember to laugh. The laughter got me through a lot, more than you or your cousins would ever want to know. Your girls love your belly laughs, your colleagues love when you laugh at your own jokes. When you laugh you release tension. I don't know what it is, but there is something healing about laughing."

Aunty then told me a couple of Goan folklores to ease my mind about never listening to my mother about them. She talked about Devchars who are spirit-Gods and how he was stuck in a bottle, about a princess with beautiful blond hair who caused her life to change dramatically because she didn't listen to her parents, and about the bond between the guardian deity, Ravanath and the Goan people. The Goan have affection for the od, but also fear Revanath. I pondered those stories, tried to search for the meanings of all of them, and thanked my Aunt for telling me those fables.

After a long pause, I tried to go back and ask what the other turning points were, but you could tell she did not want to tell me. Aunt Kathy took the last sip of her straight whiskey and said. "My time here is done, I must get back to heaven. Don't give up, remember you grew out of your shy shell. Think of what you want and you will get it." With that, she hugged me and bid me farewell.

The next day, I had several relatives that came into the viewing area. Both sets of grandparents, my Uncle Mike, Aunt Phylis, Uncle Donald, Uncle AJ, Uncle Normie, and my Aunt Kathy were all there. It is funny as I never met my mom's dad or my uncle Mike. My grandfather Rodriguez had my look. He was bald, tan skin, brown eyes, and could only grow a light beard. I wanted to talk to him and ask him questions, but this was not the place. My Uncle Mike died of cancer well before I was born. It was not a conversation my father ever really brought up. Phylis, AJ, and Normie were my dad's uncles/ aunts. However, when we went to reunions in the 1,000 islands and Minnesota, they were especially pleasant. AJ always loved playing his fiddle. He still wears his red trucker ball cap too.

Before we started, a man in a priest garb approached me. Even though he spoke slowly, he didn't let formalities like a hello interrupt his thought process and started right away to tell me God has always been with me and to believe in myself. "Be the student I knew you were." Then I realized it was Father Doyle who taught me several

Political Science classes at college. "You studied hard, you earned your grades, you never let anyone down. Do not let yourself down and know the man you really are. Your life was not a dream, keep the faith." I thanked him and went to sit down on the last bench in the visitors' gallery. I wondered if Sister Christopher from Kennedy Middle would be next. She would sit in the front of our classroom and have us come up one by one and read our grades out loud with critique. She made my core mental strength stronger by doing that. Alas, she never showed up.

"Good morning, your honors," said proudly by Ms. Jenkins

"We would like to call up Sophia Riley."

"Objection, can we approach the bench, your honors?" shouted Mr. Davis

"Both lawyers may approach," bellowed Judge Wapner

"Your honors, I know that Ms. Riley and Mr. McNab have seen each other and she could be compromised."

Ms. Jenkins admitted that I did see her, how she argued that we had no intentions of calling her up. "Chuck never knew that he should refrain from talking to past friends who might be called to the witness stand. It was highly unusual for two people to find each other up here as well."

That's Sophia for you, always finding a way to get things to happen.

Judge Ginsberg spoke privately with Judge Wapner. Then, Judge Wapner spoke, "We would like to privately talk with Ms. Riley in my office. The court is at recess for 15 minutes.

Ms. Riley

"**M**s. Riley, what type of conversation did you have with Mr. McNab when you saw him the other day?"

"I gave him a tour, told him how to know when a local passes away and talked about my family."

"Anything about his case?"

"No, nothing about it."

"Ms. Riley, do you want Mr. McNab to go to heaven?"

Absolutely, if he deserves it. He is a nice guy and always has the best for his community. I don't know his outside life, you would know that your honors. All I know is what he did at school.

Alright, we will make our ruling in a few minutes. Please leave us to chat Ms. Riley.

Ruth did not hesitate or jumbo her words as she spoke. She was calm as well.

Yes, she definitely was not flustered. I believe she will be a credible witness and will give fair, honest answers.

Court resumes

———— ⁓ ————

Judge Wapner came in and ruled that Ms. Riley make be called up to testify.

Ms. Jenkins asked Ms. Riley to state her name and how she knew me. Sophia responded back with her name and that she was a clerical at the same school.

How long did you know my client?

Oh, Chuck hired me. About 4 years.

I originally interviewed for his personal clerical position, but that was not offered to me. Instead, he hired me for a job that he thought suited me better.

Does Chuck know your husband?

Yes, he has helped Chuck with some odd jobs.

Does Chuck know that one of your relatives is a School Board member?

Yes, everyone did..

Chuck had to be pretty secure with himself not to give you the first job?

I suppose so. I know he did what was right for the building. He also does what is right for the building, staff, and especially the kids.

Would you say that Chuck is well respected by the staff and that he has a lot of friends in the building?

Absolutely! He is always chatting with someone. It is extremely rare that a negative is said about him. The only times you hear is when Dino and Chuck are fighting.

Fighting?

Yeah, on what is best for the building.

Chuck needs to be pretty secure in himself to fight with his boss, correct?

"Objection, leading the witness," stated Mr. Davis.

"Overruled," said Judge Ginsburg

Honestly, Chuck will stand up to whomever if he will make a difference for the kids.

Is there a time he could have lost a lot of friendships, but still chose to follow the path that was in the best interest of kids?

When I first got there, there was hoopla about 21 different teachers moving their classrooms. Chuck had this idea that the team teachers should be near each other. It would reduce the amount of time in the hallways for the kids and that the teachers could communicate with each other. You would have to understand that several teachers were in the classrooms for over 15-20 years. This was a veteran staff. No one takes kindly to change.

Chuck presented his case to the teachers union, department chairs, and faculty. He offered meetings with departments and with individual teachers. If he heard a good idea or was able to make something happen that got another person OK with the shift, he did it. He risked a lot of friendships to do what is right for his kids.

No more questions your honor.

Sophia did very well defending my approach. Mr. Davis even remarked that she made my advocate's case of this point. Now it was my turn.

"I would like to call Chuck up, your honors."

"Chuck, what do you say about the claims that you are insecure about friendships?"

"I would agree. However, it is what I am have grown to understand through my environment. I wonder if Mr. Davis, would you rather have someone who doesn't care about friendships or someone who cares as much?"

"Objection, the witness cannot pose question to opposing counsel."

"Overruled, it wasn't formed as a question. Continue, Ms. Jenkins."

"Chuck, what did your assistant superintendent say to you about friendships and your job?"

A lot of people have said that we are expendable. Once we leave, someone else will move in like nothing ever happened. I did not want them. Not to say I wanted to be a savior, but I hope I left a positive impression in people's minds when I leave. Friendship at work fades away when someone is promoted or moves on to another position.

The reflecting that you do, is it about all friends or work friends?

Sometimes, I would think about any friend. Like my friend Vanessa, who basically isolated herself from us when she was getting divorced from a dirtbag. Sorry for my language your honors. I felt bad for her, but there was no way to communicate. I would reflect, but after a while that went away. This Christmas she wrote, but I didn't see the need to respond. Ms. Jenkins, maybe it is just me, but I don't want to be just anyone who people are like Ok. Most of my reflection comes from my friends at work. Am I too much of a friend, too little? Am I putting too much into it? Are they putting anything into it? Do they care? This is especially the case for people who were close, but have moved on. I do my breaths when something gets in my mind. That helps me settle down and realize I am thinking way too much into something. So, I have been working on it.

As for your heritage, what is your favorite type of food?
Indian
"Are you teaching your girls all their backgrounds?"
"Yes, Lisa and I believe it is important for them to know it and I do not want them doing the same mistake I did."
"I rest with this witness, your honors."
"May I ask one question?" stated Mr. Davis
"Proceed."
"You admit you are insecure with friendship?"
"With certain work friendships, yes."
"So you are saying you are insecure with friendships?"
"With certain work friendship."
"Please answer the exact question."
"Your honors, the witness has answered the question."
"I agree, he has."
"Then, I am all set."
"In five minutes, we will start closing arguments."

Closing Arguments

M s. Jenkins said she was all set. She was going to talk with Mr. Davis to see who would go first. She walked over there and they were discussing, but the facial expressions appeared that they did not agree with themselves. After a while, Mr. Davis took a coin out and there was a flip. Ms. Jenkins said something and they watched as the coin spun on the floor. Then Mr. Davis did a small fist pump to the sky. Ms. Jenkins walks back over and says we are going first. She told me to relax because she has this. As she approached the judges, she looked them in the eyes and her body language displayed confidence.

"Hello, your honors. No matter what Mr. Davis says after I finish, I will not be able to rebuttal him as he will speak last. When he presents his argument, please put yourself in my place and wonder how I would have countered his perspective.

Mr. McNab will never get to dance with his daughters again.

Mr. McNab will never get to say I love you to his wife again.

Mr. McNab will never get the chance to walk his daughters down the aisle for their weddings.

Why? Because he displayed courage, compassion for others, treated others before thinking of himself, and honest in his profession by always being the ultimate warrior in support and defend his students and staff. There is no other choice, but heaven."

I was thinking to myself that was extremely short; where was the evidence, where is the…hey, it wasn't even two minutes long. Yet, the images you got from her words were powerful. I would never get to do those things. There are a lot of other things I won't be able to do as well that I always wanted to do.

Mr. Davis then stood up and with force started to drill his speech into the judges' minds.

"At the beginning of this trial, your honors, I thanked you for taking the time to listen to this case. You took time away from your family members who are in heaven because they, just like you, had clearly all four attributes that God wanted people to have to enter this privileged place. Mr. McNab has on occasion done things in each category. He has also don't things that goes against those values. I have listed several of these things, like stealing and how he treated others relationships in college. He does not deserve to be in heaven like your family members. Why drop the standards because he shot a person in his school. As his boss once said, people are expendable. The sun, moon, and the rest of the world did not stop when Mr. McNab was shot. He had a micro, microenvironment stop for a second, as his school is now reopened. Teachers teach, children learn. I might sound harsh, but Mr. McNab is a general person who helped for a day but is not a martyr. He had his demons or rather flaws that he even under oath acknowledged. Thank you again for your time."

I was choking on my fears after he spoke. Was he right? Am I going to hell? This is worst than taking those tests to get certified. I must remember that the fear of the unknown is worse than the reality. I took four deep breaths and prayed to God.

The Waiting

The waiting felt like days, but it was hours. My advocate was upset though as things never went this long. She called her supervisor, but he said we should hang on tight and that this is a unique situation. Ms. Jenkins told me that murderers, child abuse perps, and hostage holders usually do not even leave the room after the closing arguments. Plea deals are usually during the last recess, but I was not offered one. That means it is all or nothing. I should have asked Ms. Jenkins why a plea was not offered. I mean I would have done a few years here to get into heaven. I play the safe bet, not the all-in bet. I would have totally have been OK with a plea since I know I was nowhere close to perfect.

Ms. Jenkins, I have a question. How many trials are going on at the same time? I have been thinking about this since we started.

Well, Chuck, 100s of trials are going at the same time.

Then, how did I get three high-profile judges?

So, that is a good question. Usually, certain judges are used less frequently. They are either for extremely important cases or to help out when there is an issue. Just like how Judge Taft had to leave to help another case, that is what one of these three would normally do. I have never seen all three together. It was like an All-Star game where you had the best at all bases.

I was about to grab a hot dog when both Ms. Jenkins and I got a notice on our arms to report back to the chambers.

The Walk

I asked Ms. Jenkins if I could make a quick call before I go back to the courthouse. She had told me prior that once they make the decision there is no time for anything else. With these payphones, you can call phone numbers down below to Earth to hear people's voices. The people down below will think they are scams, such as having a car warranty that is about to expire or credit card fraud. I guess those are not the most pleasant calls, but you get to hear their voices and sometimes they make some funny voices. My daughter took one out of my playbook and said that she is going to charge $1 a minute and that she needed my credit card number to charge me. Shane had told me that people also use these phones to call people to change a series of events. That actually happened to me twice during an interview. Well, I dragged my feet long enough. It was awesome hearing her voice and hopefully, that won't be the last time I hear it. In heaven, you can hear their voices. All the times I heard them, I mute the fighting.

I fear that my girls would someday associate me with Cecile in One Crazy Summer. In the book, the mother was a mother in name only. She was selfish and did whatever pleased her. She left them and moved from Brooklyn to Oakland never to remember them. She couldn't even say the youngest child's name as she despised it. I don't want my girls to think of me as a selfish, deadbeat father. Maybe I will be like Lincoln. It is said the train bringing his corpse along the Hudson River still makes an appearance on that anniversary night followed by union soldiers. Would it be creepy if I did that at my school? Then my daughters would be able to see me. Enough of that. Think positive like Lisa would say.

Verdict

⌘

Ms. Jenkins told me to pray and to thank the judges before they place a verdict. She explained that if I am sentenced to hell, I will have to go to the door on my left where the bailiff with tats all over his arms was. I did exactly as she asked me to do. In my mind, I repeated a prayer that would help me stay peaceful. "God, grant me the serenity to accept the things I cannot change, courage to change the things I can, and wisdom to know the difference".

Ms. Jenkins still motioning with her hands continued to say "Heaven you go to the room on your right. There are no appeals in the decision."

As the judges entered the courtroom I was thinking of the Darius Rucker song, "I'm going straight to hell", we all stood and I asked if I can say something for a moment. Judge Ginsberg allowed me to speak, but I just had to wait until the stenographer was ready. Once she was, I thanked the judges for their time away from their families and appreciated the fair trial. Judge Ginsberg added that they took my question very seriously about Judge Taft leaving. However, that was a little part of their decision. She then added that hell would not be an option for me. I actually thought that when doing a verdict a judge would just say what it was, but it was almost as if they were going in slow motion to cause suspense. Ms. Jenkin was already happy though because no hell meant she won the case in some way. Judge Ginsberg then added that probation to be served in purgatory would not be an option as well. Couldn't they just say I was going into heaven! I almost started bouncing up and down. I couldn't contain my excitement. Then Judge Ginsberg stated they were giving me a choice. Huh? The judges could see that both Ms. Jenkins and I were confused. For that matter, Mr. Davis was confused.

Judge Wapner then started to speak.

"This was a very unique case. One that neither of us has ever had to listen and make a verdict on. The case presented to us, if it was clear and simple, we would say you could go to heaven and we still say you can go to heaven if you choose. However, right from the start as you walked to the entry gate, you were never slated to be here at this time. The entry gate, hotel, even this trial was sudden notice. Taft, Ginsberg, and I were supposed to be on break until January. However, when God needs a favor we all jumped in. It seems Taft helped God twice this week. That brings me to Taft. He left. Again, if there was any small doubt about going to heaven, your research into this would have compelled us to let you go into heaven, however, that was not needed. We are going to give you a choice."

Wait, I am getting a choice. What is going on?

"You can choose to go to heaven or choose to go back with your family on Earth. We believe that there is a lot more for you to do down on Earth and a lot more students who need you to impact their future. We are going to take a recess and in 10 minutes you will have to make a decision."

What are the odds? I never thought I would see my L and kids again except through these channels. That hole in my heart is filling rapidly like I struck oil. Wait, take four deep breaths and face reality. Let me see what Ms. Jenkins has to say by I should study all my options.

Ms. Jenkins and I stepped out into the hallway and sat on one of the benches near a vending machine. Ms. Jenkins then explained further the pros and cons of each choice. However, in my mind, this was a huge, hard decision. Heaven with family or family that I never got to say goodbye to.

Ms. Jenkins stated, "The pros with heaven is that you are reunited with your family, you can look over your family on Earth, you are assured heaven which is not always easy, and you can live in paradise. I have yearned for that day, Chuck. The pros of Earth is that you can finish all the goals that you had planned, you can be with your family enjoying birthdays, Christmas, and being present in the moment. I do wish I still had that experience."

She concluded with "I don't know if that helped. In the end, it is your choice. If you choose Earth, you heard what the judge said about heaven in the future."

"If I choose Earth, how would my paperwork be flagged for what the judges said?"

"You have an angel that look over you. Until you get to heaven you won't see it, but will make sure you are protected."

We went back into the courthouse and it was time to give my decision. I am at that fork in the road like Robert Frost stated in his famous poem. Judge Wapner asked me to stand up and pledge that the decision I came up with was done by free will. Then he asked for it. I immediately thanked the court again and thanked Ms. Jenkins. Then I stated, "I want to go back to Earth. I want to helped Madison learn how to read, Nicole work on her competition swim meets, eventually get them through college, and see them both get married. I would like to be a grandfather someday and be in their lives. I want to grow old with Lisa and travel the world like we started to do when we got married. I have a lot of wants, I have a lot of dreams, and they all take place on Earth. I appreciate the court helping me when I return, but I hope it is a long way off." I guess I took the road less traveled by as most people who were at the goal line would jump into the endzone instead of voluntarily going back to the 50. However, my 50-yard line was my happiness which will produce a lot of first downs.

Judge Ginsberg noted my decision and stated that the transition will happen right away. Then she gave some advice.

"You have a great head on your shoulders. You do a lot for your students and you provide well for your family. You need to ease up on yourself, live in the moment, and believe in yourself. Own your story, don't worry about others and you will live whole heartening. I noticed that you used to do mindfulness. Ironically, the stress on the pandemic caused you to stop. You need to clear the part, be still, and it will help with the angst. Remember in the movie, For the Love of the Game, when Costner was pitching and he blocked out all the noise? Mindfulness did that for him. When you work, when you don't sleep because you want to get ahead of your work, you become less valuable and opposite of what you believe. You need that calmness back in your life and enjoy those everyday moments. Losing sleep because you live in fear of the future is not healthy, you can't enjoy the present. So, get out of that tunnel vision. The last thing I want to caution you about is taking everything you heard here and thinking you must be perfect."

"Excuse me, your honor, will I remember all of this?"

Judge Wapner explained "It will be the furthest part of your memory. You might see a picture and suddenly a thought will come into mind, but you will not understand why."

Judge Ginsburg then interjected, "As I was saying, I used to try to be perfect when I was fighting the institutions who held women down. However, there is always a crack in the perfect world. That crack might offer you light and guidance. When you have flaws, you can grow or sudden surprises might turn out positive. At the end of the day, you have character flaws like us all, but know you have a tremendous amount of good and we applaud you and your decision."

Then she made a similar comment that Ms. Jenkins did earlier. "You probably won't automatically go to heaven the next time you are here. People that are automatic are Sister Theresa types. However, if you are equivalent to what you are now though, Wapner and I will seal the approval of heaven without a prolonged trial. The next time you come up here you will arrive at our chamber, we will look over the notes, and if everything looks fine, you will immediately go into heaven. If there are any red flags, you will stand trial."

"Mr. McNab, the court and staff bid you farewell. Please exit through the doors in the back and someone will escort you to the train."

My family members had tears in their eyes. I couldn't go see them, but my grandpa looked at me with his crystal blue eyes and a smile on his face. My Aunt Kathy blew me a kiss, and both my grandmas smiled and waved.

Wow, I am going home. I had two songs playing in my head at the same time. "For the first time" by Darius and "I get Knocked Down" by Chumbawamba replayed repeatedly. The lines of the songs started to blend together, but it made a beautiful melody in my head.

At the train depot

At the train depot, I was still in shock. Who would have imagined all these curves? Literally, five minutes after the trial was over, I was boarding the train. They had to find a conductor that was certified in this subway train. It was one of the number 7 red subway cars we used to find in the city. My mom and I would sometimes let other subway trains pass by just so we could get on a red car. There was nothing special inside, but just being on it felt like a million bucks. I think 15 years ago they dumped the last one in the Long Island Sound. Ms. Jenkins told me they finally found someone from heaven that used to be an NYC conductor to drive the train. They had let the last person go to heaven after years of service in purgatory. Even though we could dress however we like, he was determined to get his old uniform back on with the black hat. He reminded me of the city and my love for the subways. I wonder if this will park in one of the old subway tunnels not being used anymore. All those classic stops were not being used because the platform was either too small or they created more advanced stops nearby. The city hall stop is still one of the most beautiful stations ever created. I always wondered if they opened those old stops back up and created stores or event areas and how it would add element to New York City. The conductor said all abroad and we proceeded to gain movement. The next thing I knew we were at the old train station for FDR and the Waldrof hotel. The train he used is still there abandoned. The steel looks like it has not been touched since 1945. I step out of the number 7 train and I stepped onto the platform. There are Coke and Mr. Pep bottles from the 1970s. I push the up button for the elevator. The button looks shining clean, but the door looks like it hasn't been touched for decades. My assumption came from the layers of dirt and dust that were splattered on there. As I open the door.....

Awake

The Days/Weeks After

⌘

The lights were starting to flash. I could feel something tugging in my arm and constantly beeping. Mixed in with the beeps was the pounding of the rain. Were the stars crying because I was dead? I need someone now to explain what is going on. I am about to burst.

"Where am I?" I shouted. A strange voice then said this is Westchester Medical Center.

"You were flown here from Danbury Hospital. I am Dr. Sanrij and my staff has been through all the ups and downs in your journey. We are all relieved you woke up. Your wife insisted you stay on the ventilator because she knew you would find a way to come back."

"Why am I here? What day is it?"

"Sir, you were shot three days ago. Once shot in the leg and another in your stomach. As you were shot, you fell down some stairs which caused internal bleeding in the head. We were able to recover the bullets and patch you back up. It was the head that kept you in this state. You were talking to yourself throughout the three days like you were in a court appearance."

"Doc, I don't know about court appearances, but I have been having wild dreams. One was I left my kids on an Amtrak as Lisa and I got off the train. When we realized it, we ran after it. The train turned in a bus and I was holding on for my dear life." As I finished that thought, my mind starting racing about my family.

"Are my kids alright?"

"Yes and your wife as well. Plus, you are a hero as you saved your school from having more injuries."

"What do you mean?"

"You stopped a cold-blooded killer and you saved your staff and students. Even though we are in Westchester, the Putnam County Sheriffs have had an officer here watching over you till you recovered. A deputy name Hunter is here as well."

"Hunter….why do I remember that name?"

"Your memory might have been affected during this ordeal. Some things will come back quickly, while others will be slower. Deputy Hunter said he worked with you, do you want your first visitor?"

"Sure."

"Charles McNab, you are awake."

"I think so. You are Deputy Hunter? Am I in trouble?"

"Well, no one pranked your room while you were gone if that is what you mean?"

"Pranks?"

"You loved pulling and receiving pranks. I am going to call Kathy to let her know you are awake and I will be back. You know what? I will just text her. I am sorry this had to happen. I wish I was at the school."

"I am sure you are dedicated. I don't remember the whole situation, but I am guessing it wasn't good."

"Well, turn on any local news channel or better yet, I can YouTube CBS news when they aired this. Hell, I can turn on CNN because you made them as well, even though I can't stand CNN. Buddy, you are a national hero."

Watching what CNN, Fox News, and other filmed the day and days after the event, I was a mix of emotion. The bottom line is I probably saved others' lives. I also almost lost my daughters' father and Lisa's husband. Thinking this, I really want to see Lisa and the girls. I want their hugs, kisses, and just to hear their voices.

The next morning, I actually woke up to what seemed to be hundreds of flowers and balloons. However, the most valuable items in there were watching me sleep, which was my family.

"Lisa, I thoughtit was only one visitor at a time for COVID."

"Do you think they were going to mess with me? When they said that, I used your Twitter account and publicly messaged Cuomo. He personally called the hospital and told them to test us right away and then to admit the family."

"Awesome thinking, Lisa. Well, Cuomo needs a little positive rating right now. He is tanking as much as Trump."

"Lisa, I am sorry…"

"For what? You knew this day might come in the back of your mind. You plan lockdowns, you plan safety, those kids and staff are under your umbrella when they are with you. I am sorry you had to do it, but everyone present said you acted calm, rational, and tried other tactics before you were shot. I would only hope my principal or assistant principal would do that if our school was ever in a crisis."

"Daddy, daddy"

"Madison, give me a big hug."

"Can I give you an Eskimo kiss as well? I have missed those."

"Sure, but it Samosa kiss, daddy, how could you forget?"

"Nicole, why are you crying like you lost your puppy?"

"Daddy, I misssssed you. Mommy told us you were on a business trip, but I knew something was wrong….I knew she was lying. Dadddddy, I am soooo happy."

"Come over here, everything is going to be all right."

"Just then Doctor Evans came into the room."

"Excuse me, I just got word you have a phone call that is urgent."

"Lisa, who could that be?"

"Chuck, I don't know….Let me go check."

Really...

———— ❦ ————

"**D**octor, I don't know if Chuck can really take any phone at the moment."

"I know, but I can't say no to this person"

Really....I can."

"Maam, it is President Trump. He is bragging that a principal in his home state saved lives."

"Doctor, didn't he switch residency to Florida?"

"Ma'am, you and I both know that, but what can you say, this is Trump. He also wants to do a video chat. We can connect it to our zoom link."

"I will let Chuck know. Also, for the sake of my girls, I don't want any cameras in the room and none of his aides."

"Alright, I will tell them just that."

Lisa came back into the room and told me what was going on. How could I pass up talking to the president of the United States? I loved to write to celebrities and sports players to get their autographs. I have two of his, but I can't seem to hang them on the walls. They are gently placed in my storage area next to Rudy's autograph when he was mayor.

Hello

✏

"Hello, I am President Trump. Who are these good-looking ladies?"

"This is Nicole, this is Madison, and I am Lisa."

"I'm delighted to meet you, Lisa."

"Mr. President, my husband is tired. I appreciate that you are checking in on him, but my job now is to protect him. My job is to make sure he gets his rest and the care needed to be here for our family. So, not to be rude, but please make this quick."

"I don't remember a lady ever talking to me like that. I like it. So domineering. Look, I wanted to congratulate someone who would risk his life in a school building for all his kids and staff."

"Mr. President..."

"Lisa, you may call me Donald."

"Donald, we know you...."

"I love Trump," said Madison interjected."

Lisa never got to finish her sentence. She was getting angry and God helps anyone who crossed her.

"Charlie, were you able to vote? If not, I will get Rudy to file a petition to let you vote late and express what all those real voters expressed."

"Anyway, Charlie is a hero. I love heroes. I am a hero myself. We heroes need to still together, especially in the great state of New York."

"Lisa, have you ever seen Trump's tower? Do you want to get a personal tour?"

It seemed that he was started to flirt with my beautiful blonde delight. However, she wasn't taking any bait. You have to wake up pretty early to outwit her sharp mind.

"Our family would love a personal tour. Right girls?

"Yeah!"

"Ummm....sure the family can have a personal tour. Charlie, how are you? I almost forgot why I came here." He laughed nervously when he said this.

"I am good, Mr. President. Thank you for asking."

"Well, if I ever get back up to that area of yours, I want to play a little golf in my Hopewell location anyway. I still have a park up there named after me, right? It doesn't matter, I am honored with what you did. You are a brave man. I would like to present you with a medal for your bravery at the White House. Would you be interested?"

"Absolutely...where would we stay though when we get down there?"

"My travel secretary will arrange it."

"Daddy, do you remember the American girl store? They have one down there."

"If your girls love that store, the first lady can take them shopping."

"Wow, that would be awesome."

"Mr. President, can I ask a favor?"

'Want me to fire someone? I am very good at that?"

"No, can you also invite Deputy Hunter from the Putnam County Sherriff's department as well? Hmm....I don't see why not...."

"Maybe your secret service and contract with his department for his services throughout the whole trip. This way he doesn't lose any potential overtime. He is saving for his wedding."

"That's fine. We will see to it. Alright, I got to run. I have to make sure I have time to work on my putting. Also, I have a state park named after me in Yorktown. Great photo op. They named the parks after me because I am great. Do any other living presidents have that? No, no they don't. So long and in a couple of days, we will see each other again. By the way, as a citizen, should I fire Barr? He argues with me and doesn't do what I want."

"Sir, you know better than I do, but with a month left in office, is it worth it?"

"A Month? No, I won the election. Hmmm....so what I am hearing, is it is worth it? I should fire him, good idea. I should tweet this. Let's take a picture first over zoom. Doc, come in here. As a first responder, I would love you to join. Thanks. Bye girls!"

"You know Chuck, if I had known he was coming, we probably would have to be tested."

"You are so right. I am glad he wore his mask most of the time."

Madison loves him. The big hug she gave him when he left was priceless. The girls being able to see the White House would be a once-in-a-lifetime opportunity. Sue Kelly once allowed me to take the seniors there. I had one student who did not have a social security number so he had to wait outside. I gave up my opportunity to go in, but after a while, the secret service agent asked if I could couch for him and I said yes. He allowed us to race through the White House to catch up to the group. It is funny, I remember that conversation more than I remember the inside of the White House. We couldn't go to the Oval that day because Bush was using it. All in all, it was well worth it.

Daddy, I am just excited about the American Girl store.

Me too!

I know girls. You two may see the new girl of the year, whoever she is.

Doctor's prognosis

~~~

Y ou certainly made a fast recovery after waking up. Your vitals are good. There is feeling in both your legs and your mind is not as fogging as it was. We will be discharging you soon, but be mindful to take it slowly. If you go too fast, you may reinjure yourself or may face other complications. I will need you to start doing Physical Therapy and they will guide you for how long. I would recommend acupuncture as it is fantastic with these types of ailments. So remember to move slowly, don't exert too much energy, and try to be stress-free. Does this guy know me? I am stressing by not being able to play with my kids, too take a shower by myself, basically do anything by myself.

Doc, when will I be able to be independent?

Like I said, it will take time and the PT person will better guide you with that.

When will I be able to work?

Honestly, I wouldn't recommend you give the speech, but you will anyway. Take gradual steps. We will follow up in 3 weeks. If you need anything my nurse will give you the after hour's number. I got discharged and was allowed to go home.

The hospital attendant takes me in a wheelchair to the ramp waiting for Lisa to drive the car over. Madison was in her car seat and Nicole was sitting in the 3rd row of our Subaru. Not much talking was going on in the front row. Nicole was reading a book and Madison was asking for a puppy. L and I just held our hands together like we did on our wedding day. I could recall on that day that she wasn't the one crying like a baby while trying to say the vows, but me. Instead, she held my hand and gently massage it to assure me that everything was good. She must have gotten the sense that everything that just happened must have engulfed me. I do enjoy the quietness; sometimes being quiet is in fact loud. I heard Madison clearly expressing the type of dog she wanted I could hear Nicole turn the pages, and I even heard the bus pass us by. She was driving like I did when we brought Nicole home for the first time; 35 in a 55. In this case, she was doing 50 in a 65 where everyone was doing 80. The Westchester County police must have a field day on this road like a cat in a room with a box of mice.

When I got home, Madison asked if we could eat in the basement while we watched a movie. We let Nicole pick a Marvel movie and ate the mouth-watering Tanjore Indian food while the girls ate mac and cheese. We went through the motions after that with having bath time, singing the songs, and tucking in the girls for bed. However, it wasn't just a routine. I sang the songs with passion, I felt the softness of the linen, and I noticed how high the bubbles got in the tubs prior to the girls jumping into their respective tubs.

Lisa and I finally went to our room. I pulled the Bible out of the nightstand. Lisa looked at me inquisitively and I explained I was searching why God gives second chances; I was wondering why I was able to come back from near death. It took me a while, but I found it. Mr. Buckley from Kennedy Catholic would have been proud. "God savors opportunities to offer second chances and is eager not to punish us when we truly seek forgiveness for our sin" (Joel 2:13). Reflecting on that and other verses I read that night, I realized that my pathway was still under construction and I had more to provide in the world. I had a second chance to complete my goals. As we kissed good night, I apologized for not watching the girls that day. I won't take for granted our partnership. Family first.

D.C.

$\mathcal{CP}$

We took a train to DC since Lisa did not want to fly as it was raining pretty furiously. This tin can of a car was dripping. Lisa questioned me why we did not take the Acela and I assured her that on the way back we would. Trump or Biden should invest more into the Amtrak system. There are areas like Nashville that are not connected. There are routes that if upgraded, more people would use them which would reduce car emissions. We need to replicate what France or Japan have. We are not just discussing the North East, but the Midwest as well. Imagine a train system that connected all Major League baseball teams. That would be a home run. How about an underground train to Hawaii? That might be more of a risk, but dreams do become reality. I spent the next few hours working on my speech. Trump's people wanted it ahead of time, but I just did not have time. As I was working on it, the girls were plastered to the windows looking at anything that went by. From the water to the towns and to the state of disrepair of what DC looks like. This reminds me of the bathroom at Wendy's in DC when I took my seniors to the White House. They had to get dressed from their pajamas to formal clothes so we stopped at Wendy's. The bathroom was locked with a chain and padlock and you needed to get the key from the counter. The restaurant looked like it was going through a war zone. I was really hoping that DC would have improved by then.

We arrive at Union Station. Immediately, the girls started starving. It isn't like they had raided the café on the train. However, we stop at Johnny Rockets. This particular one is always small and dirty, but their shakes were incredible. This location made me think of the days when smoking was allowed and you could envision the cook smoking while frying burgers. While eating lunch, Deputy called Pauline and you could hear her upset that she could not come along. He explained again that the Sheriffs were hired to have someone escort us to the White House. She could read between the lines though. She wasn't happy.

We head upstairs to the rental company when a group approached us in suits. It was representatives from the White House taking us in a limo to the Trump International Hotel. I thought the Travel Secretary was going to book us in the Ritz like we asked. He did…then the president found out and canceled it. The hotel itself is very beautiful. I believe it used to be a post office before becoming a hotel. We unpacked, settled in, and do a family walk around the hotel. We love to go into empty conference rooms and see what is going on. If this was during baseball season, we would make sure to stay at a hotel that the players were at so we can scout for autographs. After the hotel walk, we took a walk outside. Of course, the kids were hungry, so had to get back to the hotel. Even at a fancy restaurant, Madison wanted mac and cheese while Nicole ordered chicken tenders. The difference between Perkins mac and cheese and this restaurant was the price tag. They both use Kraft. One charges $4 while the other charges $12. I guess it is because you get to use a fancy fork. We realized how late it was getting and we start our bathroom time routine. Once in bed, I started reading a book to Madison and while doing so, I drifted away thinking about how special this is, how special we as humans can connect with our loved ones. She was just smiling, laughing, trying to say the words on the page by herself. We need to soak those precious moments up because they are short-lived. Once the girls were put to sleep, I looked at my speech. I had done speeches for board members and for conferences, but this will be the biggest speech in my life.

President Trump had us in the rose garden. No one was social-distancing and only a few had their masks on. But I figured that for a five-minute speech on safety in the schools, I could deal with it. My family found seats far enough from the people not wearing masks. In fact, one person did not have one on and Madison asked him to do so. I think it was a Congressman she boldly told to do that. No, it was Senator Cruz.

"Good morning my fellow Americans and thank you to President Trump for letting me speak on safety in schools. First, I must say thank you to all the hard-working administrators and staff that dedicate their time, energy, and resources in making schools a success no matter the type of environment. Today, our students are witnessing violence that other generations have not experienced. There is roughly 29 violent incidents per 1,000 students. 80% of our kids said they have experienced one or more intolerable, unsafe acts while in school. We need to ensure a safe environment for our students. However, it wouldn't be a surprise to see an attack on other students, teachers, or other staff. When I was teaching, I once saw a mother come in to yell at the principal and then shoved her in the hallway to get to a kid that was picking on her child. I had a parent sneak into our cafeteria from a meeting to holler at a child for calling her child ugly. By the way, the child texted his mom about the incident and she came in to defend him. Whoever witness these type of acts can start to feel anxiety which deepens the social-emotional stress we are noticing in schools. More mental health is needed in our schools, but unfortunately, we are cutting more resources. When you start to cut personnel, more violence will occur. Take for example a 1st grader in Michigan who shot and killed another 1st grader. Another example is a 14-year old child who was suspended. The next day, he comes to the building and kills 2 teachers and 2 students besides himself. Having a universal mental health screener in the building that can detect issues that students might have is crucial. Then having personnel to support them is necessary. This could be school staff or a partnership with a clinic that comes to use our building after school. A partnership with outside therapy can benefit everybody. It would benefit the 55% of LGBT students that report they have been cyberbullied. It would help the students who feel isolated and others who are a high risk for suicidal behaviors. Finally, not every student succeeds in a large public school. Creating alternative programs that reduce the number of students and provide a therapeutic setting can benefit at-risk students. Please join me, the members of Congress and Mr. Trump in supporting our future by giving them the resources they need to be successful."

As I finished, Mr. Trump squeezed my back and told me he was so proud of me. He said, "You just helped my ratings." I was staring at him thinking the president was complimenting and how honored I was to give a speech at the White House. My family was clapping and the President gave some closing remarks. Afterwards, we got to have coffee and pastries in the Roosevelt room. Tom was talking about weddings. He was still trying to find a location. He had proposed in the Bronx Gardens but wanted something closer to home for the actual wedding. I had suggested Locust Grove as it is a beautiful, historical spot in Dutchess. From there, the travel secretary came over to let us know that we would first take a tour of the White House, pictures in the Oval, and then to the American Girl store with the first lady. Afterwards, we would get a tour of DC and stops along the way.

The tour of the White House was incredible. The portraits of all Presidents, especially Teddy Roosevelt and Ike Eisenhower were powerful. Madison loved Washington because he looked funny with the hair, and when the tour guide discussed the wooden teeth, she started to laugh. She told the guy not to lie about who would have wooden teeth. Nicole loved how Lincoln was looking like he was thinking. Lisa was impressed that each president had their own dining ware. Couldn't they save money by using the same ones? I always thought the White House collected the paintings and sculptures, but it was not until the Kennedy administration that established the collection. The White House has over 35 bathrooms, 412 doors, a bowling alley, and 28 fireplaces! It is so big. It was valued at over $400 million. TR, who was my favorite president is the one who coined the term "White House." He came to find out that presidents are required to pay for meals, events, and even transportation. Bill Clinton was in debt because of it. Two presidents died here as well. After we went to the Oval Office to take more pictures with President Trump, we went to their secret chocolate shop so the girls could pick out what they wanted to eat. Then we were off to the American Girl Shop with the first lady. She was so nice. We got to ride in the limo with her and she spoke about her son and how Nicole would like him. She wanted to know everything about the girls; from their favorite colors to what they think a leader is. Nicole talked her ear off, but she either enjoyed it or pretended to. Madison just wanted to hug her and she let her. She said she always wanted a girl. The American Girl store was completely closed for us. They had employees open the doors and Mrs. Trump held my daughters' hands inside and told the girls to pick out whatever they wanted since she had the credit card. Lisa thanked her but said "please have some perimeters" as they might buy the whole store. She laughed and said, "Don't worry about it." They ran to the new American girl Kira doll. Mrs. Trump went and helped them choose different outfits. She even asked them what furniture they wanted. Madison picked Melody's kitchen set and Nicole picked Courtney's bed. These dolls had more accessories than my daughters do and it was incredible. We thanked Mrs. Trump and then she was actually going to take a tour with us of D.C. She first took us to the Capital. The Rotunda was incredible. Gerald Ford's statue looked just like him. The Capital was stunning and looked like something from Rome. The family took a picture up the stairs and met Schumer, our senator. He wanted a photo op which we obliged him on. He asked us if there was anything we wanted to change in New York. I wanted a better train system that connected more towns and reestablish the route that connected Beacon to Danbury. I also dreamed of our population increasing, instead of people and congressional seats leaving our great state. The girls wanted to go to school every day.

We went to the Smithsonian. Since there are so many museums, we told the girls to only pick 1 or 2 to go to. My family usually goes through a museum for 1 to 2 hours. They picked the Natural Science Museum and walked into the giant Mammoth. They wanted to see the Hope Diamond and the dinosaurs. Nicole loved all the gems. From there, they went to the Air and Space Museum. They loved the old airplanes, space shuttles, and yet still tried to get us to go to McDonald's. Mrs. Trump agreed it was time for a McFlurry. Next was Washington Monument, which had two different stones that constructed it since it was created in two different eras. The rest of the tour consisted of the Jefferson, FDR, and the spectacular MLK monument. Before we went to the Supreme Court building, we stopped at the Lincoln Memorial and the reflecting pond. The Vietnam Memorial was breathtaking as well. The girls did not quite understand it, but we explained all these names died to keep our freedom. So much history occurred here. It was an awe experience.

The Supreme Court was the last place we were going to see. We could not go into the offices, but we were able to look at other parts of the courthouse. There were pictures on the walls of former supreme court justices. The famous John Jay, Earl Warren, Ruth Ginsberg, and Willian Howard Taft to name a few. It was funny that Ginsberg and Taft were right next to each other. I almost forgot that during Taft's time, he was the chief justice appointed by Harding. What is interesting was that retired from the position 9 years later and said that he thought being a judge was better than being the president. As I looked at both pictures, I felt like they were staring back at me. Like the paintings knew me. I don't know. Maybe I need to go back to the doctor if this keeps up.

After the Supreme Court, we went back to the hotel to get our belongings. Tom bought a souvenir for Pauline's mom at the Trump store as we got into the limo. The limo had a local station playing current hits until a Maroon 5 song interrupted with a special bulletin. There were protesters at the Capital Building trying to get into the Capital. Congressmen and women were trying to find cover and the police are outnumbered. Tom asked the limo to speed to the train station. Our train was due to leave in two hours when we arrived at the station. Tom went to the counter and discussed with the agent. I don't know what he said, but he got us switched onto the Acela that was leaving in 30 minutes instead of the one we were supposed to be on. "McNab, you owe me." Since boarding was already happening, we quickly climbed on and said farewell to the District of Columbia. We were very fortunate to leave when we did as the mayor was about to put a curfew into effect. We arrived at Penn Station where our next limo from Septembre limo picked us up and first dropped Tom off before dropping my family. During the limo ride, I asked my girls what their favorite moment of D.C. was and I was surprised to hear that it was just spending time with me. Lisa and I held hands and I truly thank God for letting me live.

Mr. West

One of the many interesting conversations we had in the limo before Tom left though was about Mr. West. Mr. West survived the gunshot. I came to find out that he was in the next ER room at the first hospital. However, he was heavily guarded by Sheriffs and State Troopers. Tom told me that when the lockdown was called Sheriffs, Troopers, Brewster and even a Transit cop came to the scene. Tom had set up incident command with one of his Sergeants at the flag pole. Dino never made it to the event. Tom told me that Dino had turned his phone off to try to enjoy a day off, which I appreciated for his own sake.

The reason Tom did not go to the first hospital throughout this event was that he thought he might go against the oath he took to serve the community. That was probably a good thing for Mr. West that Tom stayed away. Tom often claimed he is one of the best at target practice. Two things he never missed was a shot and a chance to eat a donut. Once Mr. West recovered, they sent him to Sing Sing instead of the County Jail to await trial. The Sheriff thought the protection at the county jail would not suffice and that people would find a way to attack Mr. West. Once the correctional officers realized who he was, he was transferred into a cell with Big Bubba. I don't understand why Tom told me that.

His lawyer tried to claim mental insanity with the local judge, but that action was denied. Testing was allowed for mental illness. However, the testing that was requested by the defense failed to prove he was mentally ill as well since all he spoke of was how his wife was a bloodsucker and took all his worth. Too bad all this went down as he was an architect for a big firm in the city. After the jury found him guilty, he was sentenced to 20 years with a chance for parole after 15 years.

My future

When I finally got back to the school, they threw me a parade that they do for sports teams that win a division. It was covered by channel 12, one of our local stations, and even got a retired administrator to play the big drum at the end of the march. As this was still in COVID world, people lined up 6 feet apart from each other throughout the school and school property. It was a blessing to see.

I got back into my office and a colleague that I don't have the best relationship with was organizing my office. She was my clerical a long time ago and we never saw eye-to-eye. It was very nice though and she remembered how I liked to keep my desk clear and all the clutter on top of my microwave. It is silly how people think, but all my junk always ended on top of my microwave. As we were having awkward small talk, I knew she deep down still hates my personal guts. It must be rough when you are asked to be a team player and do work. The funny thing was that she loved to make grunts and slam draws when she was asked to do work that was not involving her real estate business. As this very passive conversation was taken place, a bunch of handmade cards were slid under my desk. As I was reading them from Mrs. Donohue's 7th grade class, I really felt all the love in the building. I also started to feel anxious about being back. Could I do what I did again? I almost lost my family or rather they almost lost me.

In the weeks ahead, I tried to get adjusted to work. I started to spearhead my one book, one school initiative, had a lot of parent meetings, as 20% of the students were failing. Majority never showed up to class. I even took on some of Sally's work since she just liked handy out candy which again went against district COVID policies. At a parent meeting, one mom said, "My son has his favorite chair. He sits there and plays video games and I don't know how to convince him that school matters." This was the same child who liked to flip desk when he was in school. I really wish I had classes for the parents. I believe so many students would do better socially, emotionally, and academically if the parents had a strong foundation of how to complement the school on the children's needed. We really need to develop some. I did start to socialize again, but the bagel, donuts, and other food started adding the weight back to the body. Dinokept insisting that we have working lunches where he ordered pizza almost every day. That did stop when he dropped a slice on his grey vest.

No matter how Dino, Lauren, and the rest of the school community tried to make me relaxed, I never could get as comfortable as I once was. I started to see Dr. Dawn more often. Those conversations clearly shifted from the original conversation to how I survive now in the building. My heart started to pump fast when the greeter told me there was an angry parent at the door. I would internally panick if I was at recess and heard a car's engine misfire. I said to Jo outside once, after we heard Randy's old Ford Taurus try to start, "Wow, I thought it was a gunshot." She looked at me worried. That was the last thing I wanted; for my staff and friends to look at me differently.

Soon after that, I resigned from my position to take on a human resource job in a nearby district. It was a complete shock to the staff as I didn't tell one soul. The last time I told my principal, I was given the worst type of AP responsibilities within hours and lost my secretary. As far as I was concerned, he could be the last person to know. Kathy and some other staff had already resigned or retired after the shooting. Kathy told me she needed more time with sewing and watching the grandkids play hockey. Honestly, how could I blame her?

Lauren was now the second in charge of the building as the other one went on another vacation while the kids were in the building. Dino once told me he would never mess with her since she is a minority. He was burned once trying to discipline her and she pulled the race card. My feeling is, to make a person stronger you need to how boundaries and hold people accountable. He is the captain of the ship and no matter if she was using the race card, he needs to be consistent with everyone.

Technically by not holding her responsible for her actions, he was still messing with a minority by messing with me. Funny how things work. There was a difference, even though he knew I was a minority, I never used it to get out of work. He also knew me for 20 plus years, back when we were teachers together and in the boy's locker room that we called the English department. We all acted... we all bonded together. Nothing was off-limits and that made our department stronger and untouchable.

With the new job, it allowed me to spend more time with my family and always be present at the moment. I set up new hiring strategies and a recruitment plan of action. Flood the colleges for soon-to-be experts in education. Dr. Dawn thought the change in environment would also help with PTSD. Living life to the fullest never meant as much as it does now. I do miss the students, but this was the right career choice for me. I gave my softball bat to Lauren to hide under her desk if needed. She honestly was a rising star. Not because she was unofficially mentored by me, but she has the academic tools to lead a school. She needs to get seasoned, see a school in real-time, and then she will move up the ranks pretty quickly. My only concern is that we will go for the same position one day and I get screwed. That happened the last time I mentored someone and after his first year, he got the job. Life definitely has fun with you.

Lisa went back to some of her roots as well to get me in shape. We started to do Yoga every other day. It is great to have my own personal trainer, a gorgeous one at that. She then treated me as one of her old track players and got me into walking than running. Her goal is to get me to run a 5K. Not a bad goal but she is right that running can be Zen-like. Finally, she is making me eat better. After she saw the blood work from the hospital, she used some choice expletives. She removed Peanut butter cups and chocolate from my diet. The doctor had said for a few months, Lisa said longer than that. I don't think this part will last though. Lisa has a sweeter tooth than I do. She likes to share any cupcakes or whatever comes into the house. Maybe I will need to get cupcakes filled with Reese's. Just thinking about her, she will always be my go-to person. She is the right person to always talk about the right issue on my mind. We are all hard-wired to have connections with others and L and I are deeply connected. When we first started dating, Lisa once told me how she loved the fact that she knew she was my go-to girl and that I trusted her. I probably won't like what I hear most of the time, but she is about me and our family. L is the one I know I can talk to profoundly, spiritually, and emotionally while being in a safe zone.

As for the family, we started to have family dinners. Before this, we would serve food while the girls watched TV or were on social media. It helped to strengthened our connection as a family to turn off all the devices during dinner. Nicole would say in the past that she was still communicating with us through text, but that really was not connecting. Adding the face-to-face time with any interruptions was huge. It gave a sense of my time growing up around the table with my parents and my bro. The laughing, talking, occasional arguing are healthy for the soul. Passing around the food taught cooperation. Seeing the facial cues increased our awareness of each other.

Joe Biden offered me a second job as well, which was to be on his task force of school violence and safety. I meet with people from different parts of the country through zoom and his wife. Dr. Biden ran the committee. I was happy that they let me bring Deputy Hunter with me. He has so many great ideas that we didn't need a committee. Deputy could transform our safety protocols by himself and millions of children would be better off.

Last Thought From the Author

One piece of advice for my readers; if life flashes before your eyes, you are witnessing the start of your trial. Remember to be present in the moment and your trial will lead you in the right direction.

www.ingramcontent.com/pod-product-compliance
Lightning Source LLC
Chambersburg PA
CBHW060225180626
46813CB00007B/2965